JACK DOLAN

CIA

SHORT STORIES

This is a work of fiction.

9 781300 661528

SPYCRAFT

The sun dips below the horizon, casting long shadows across the Virginia countryside as Jack Dolan exits the Langley gates. Behind the wheel of his car, the familiar weight of the Agency presses down on him as the gates behind him close, but with a deep breath, the day is done.

Jack eases onto the GW Parkway, the evening rush already in full swing. A black sedan appears out of nowhere, its hood reflecting in the fading light. It matches Jack's movements. It stays close, its driver a silhouette in the rearview mirror. As they bound on the asphalt road above the stream valleys that feed the Potomac, the sedan begins to tailgate, its proximity unnerving. Jack brakes sharply, the tires squealing. The sedan swerves violently, touching the rear bumper.

Adrenaline surges through Jack. He accelerates, weaving through the thickening traffic, the black sedan a persistent predator on his tail. Jack plans how he will end this safely. He will make it to the great Mount Vernon circle where he will lose the sedan at the monument of the home of the first president.

But the black sedan makes the first move. A reckless maneuver, a calculated risk. The sedan, its front now chipped and dented by pushing Jack, attempts to squeeze him off the road. Jack spins the wheel, the tires screaming in protest as he fishtails, narrowly avoiding a head-on collision with a minivan.

He glimpses the sedan in the rearview mirror, its diplomatic plates now unreadable, disappearing into the thickening dusk. Shaken, he reverses back onto the winding river road overlooking the Nation's Capital towards the safe house in McLean, the incident replaying in his mind, his eyes rarely missing glimpses into the mirrors. The reckless aggression, the deliberate attempt to eliminate him. It wasn't an accident. The life of the spy was about playing the long-game. But had he gotten too close, too fast?

The safe house, a basic brick building nestled amongst trees backing up to Turkey Run, near the Agency, offers temporary refuge. He takes a stiff shot of whiskey, the amber liquid doing little to soothe the tremor in his hands. The taste of metal, the screech of tires, lingers in his senses. He wonders what he knows and what they think he knows.

He needs to clear his head. A simple meal, a quiet moment. The Italian Oven, a small, unassuming place near the safe house, comes to mind. He slips out, back through the trees, blending into the twilight, hoping to lose himself in the anonymity of the evening.

The restaurant feels homey, the air thick with the aroma of garlic and herbs. He seeks out the maitre d, Maria, a woman with eyes that had seen it all. "Table for one?" she asks, her voice a low rumble.

Maria, a sly smile playing on her lips, gestures towards the back. "Follow me," she says.

She leads Jack through the maze of tables, past the bustling kitchen, to a small, secluded alcove tucked away behind the wine rack. A single table, a flickering candle casts long shadows.

"Linguine vongole," he whispers.

Maria nods, a knowing glint in her eyes. "Of course," she replies, disappearing into the kitchen.

Jack settles into the solitude, the sounds of the restaurant fading into a distant hum. The linguine vongole arrives, a simple dish, perfectly executed. Garlic clams, plump and juicy, nestled amongst the pasta. He eats slowly, savoring each bite, the familiar flavors a comforting anchor in the storm of his emotions.

The tremors subside, replaced by a quiet strength. The chase, the near-miss, the chilling reminder of the dangers he faces, seem to recede, pushed aside by the simple pleasure of a well-cooked meal. He finishes his meal, the silence broken only by the gentle clinking of glasses.

As he leaves the restaurant, the night air cools his skin, he feels a sense of calm returning. The incident, the threat, had shaken him. He is a survivor, a ghost in the shadows, and he will continue to operate, his vigilance heightened, his resolve strengthened.

The town lights blur as he walks back through the woods to the safe house, the aftertaste of the meal lingering, a comforting reminder of life's simple pleasures that can still be found amidst the chaos.

After a few hours of light sleep, Jack wakes as the sun is rising, follows Turkey Run with a headlamp and turns onto a small quiet street that leads right to the entrance gate of the Agency where the chase had begun. He needs to figure out what he knows.

The morning sun, a pale imitation of the Virginia summer heat, glinted off the glass facade of the Langley headquarters. Inside, Jack sat hunched over his desk, the hum of the Agency a constant low-grade tremor beneath the surface. His office, a cramped cubicle partitioned by flimsy sound-dampening panels, was a microcosm of the larger organization: a labyrinth of information, a hive mind buzzing with secrets.

Jack, a native of the Virginia suburbs, had grown up with the shadow of the Agency looming large. He had applied the skills of an analyst to the allure of the clandestine, joining the ranks soon after the twin towers fell and America aimed to know more about what was operating within.

His initial assignments were mundane, desk jobs analyzing satellite imagery. But Jack, with his sharp mind and an uncanny ability to connect seemingly disparate pieces of information, quickly rose through the ranks. Because of his youth in the DC area, he became the Agency's go-to expert on foreign espionage rings operating within the DC area, particularly those seeking to influence US policy on matters of national security and use the institutions of Washington.

Recently, Jack had made a significant breakthrough and he realized it must be related to what happened to him the day before. He'd uncovered a sophisticated Chinese intelligence operation utilizing Chinese nationals embedded within international organizations in Washington. These individuals, ostensibly diplomats and foreign spies, were secretly gathering intelligence, spreading disinformation, and lobbying key policymakers. The operation was subtle, insidious, a slow-burning insurgency aimed at weakening American influence through spying, counterspying, and being present at the right time.

Jack stared at the intelligence report, the threat of the Chinese operation looming large. The Taiwan issue, a constant simmering tension, had taken center stage. The Chinese government, increasingly assertive, viewed Taiwan as an inalienable part of its territory. The US, bound by treaty obligations, maintained a delicate balance, providing Taiwan with both political and military support. This delicate dance had escalated into a high-stakes game of espionage, both sides striving to outmaneuver the other, to gain an edge in the inevitable negotiations.

Jack knew the stakes were high. The Chinese operation was just one piece of a larger puzzle, a multifaceted campaign of influence and intimidation. They were probing, testing the limits, seeking to exploit vulnerabilities. He had to stay ahead of them, anticipate their moves, and protect American interests.

But the incident from the previous night, the chilling reminder of his own mortality, had shaken him. The Agency, with its layers of bureaucracy and internal rivalries, could be a tough place. Enemies lurked in the shadows, both foreign and domestic. Jack had to be vigilant, always looking over his shoulder, always questioning the motives of those around him.

He leaned back in his chair, the cool plastic a stark contrast to the rising summer heat. The hum of the Agency intensified, a cacophony of whispers, phone calls, and the clatter of keyboards. Jack closed his eyes, the weight of the world pressing down on his shoulders. He also needs to be careful and watch his own back. Ghosts were the ever-present threat of the unknown and always watching. And Jack, the ghost hunter, was ready.

The midday sun beat down on the Washington D.C. streets as Jack, disguised in a pair of faded jeans and a worn-out baseball cap, nervously adjusted the microphone hidden within the white van. He had parked discreetly on a side street, a block away from the imposing Chinese Embassy, its red walls a stark contrast to the surrounding greenery of Embassy Row. Today was the day. After weeks of meticulous surveillance and painstaking analysis, he had finally pieced together the pattern: the dead drop.

Jack glanced at his watch. The Chinese diplomat, Li Wei, a man of impeccable credentials and a notorious poker face, was due to arrive at International Park across the street, a park frequented by diplomats and in such plain sight, perhaps so plain sight, why not just do it.

Li Wei, a master of subtlety, would leave a package - the dead drop - containing sensitive information for his agent within the World Bank. Jack had been tracking Li Wei's movements for weeks, his routine meticulously observed: the daily jog, the meetings at the embassy, the occasional visit to a dimly lit Chinese restaurant on K Street. But today was different. Today, the game would change.

A black sedan, its tinted windows reflecting the sunlight, glided to a stop in front of the park. Li Wei emerged, a man of imposing stature with a steely gaze. He strolled towards a secluded bench, his movements deliberate, his eyes scanning the surroundings with practiced ease. Jack, his heart pounding, focused on Li Wei through the van's tinted windows.

Li Wei reached the bench, paused, then discreetly placed a small, intricately carved wooden bird beneath the roots of a nearby oak tree. He lingered for a moment, seemingly lost in thought, before turning and returning to his car. The sedan pulled away, disappearing down the street. Jack waited, his senses on high alert.

A wave of memories washed over him. Last year, during the IMF-World Bank Annual Meetings, he had infiltrated a high-level cocktail party, mingling among the elite economists and policymakers. He had spotted her there – Dr. Chen, a rising economist at the IMF, charming and intelligent, her laughter infectious. But beneath the veneer of professionalism, Dr. Chen harbored a dangerous secret.

She was leaking confidential data, sensitive economic forecasts, to the Chinese government. Jack had spent months meticulously documenting her activities, piecing together the puzzle, tracing the flow of information from Dr. Chen to her Chinese handlers.

The destabilizing effect of her actions was clear: subtle manipulations of economic data, the erosion of trust in international institutions, the slow, insidious weakening of economies vulnerable to Chinese influence.

Jack shook off the memory, refocusing on the present. The minutes ticked by, the silence broken only by the distant hum of traffic.

Then, a figure emerged from the shadows, a young man with a nervous demeanor, his eyes darting around suspiciously. He approached the bench, his gaze fixed on the ground. He spotted the wooden bird, hesitated for a moment, then carefully retrieved it, his fingers tracing the intricate carvings.

Jack watched, his breath held, as the young man slipped the bird into his pocket and hurried away, melting back into the nearby woods. He had seen the man before. The game had begun.

Jack slid into a booth in the bustling World Bank cafeteria, the cacophony of voices and clattering dishes a stark contrast to the hushed tones of the Agency. He surveyed the scene, a microcosm of the global community. Men and women from every corner of the globe, their faces a tapestry of cultures, engaged in lively conversations, their laughter mingling with the clinking of silverware.

A young woman in a vibrant sari discussed microfinance with a man in a crisp suit, while a group of students debated the merits of renewable energy. It was a snapshot of the world, a testament to the power of international cooperation, and a stark reminder of the forces that sought to undermine it.

Jack, however, was focused on a single objective: identifying the young man from the park, the courier who had retrieved the dead drop. He scanned the room, his gaze sharp, his mind a whirlwind of observations. He noted the subtle shifts in the crowd, the fleeting exchanges of glances, the nervous tics that betrayed underlying anxieties. But the young man remained elusive.

Suddenly, Jack spaced out. The vibrant scene in the cafeteria faded, replaced by a kaleidoscope of memories. He was back in the Virginia woods, a young boy, his eyes wide with wonder as his Scoutmaster, a gentle man with a military background, taught him the art of observation.

"The woods have eyes, Jack," the Scoutmaster had said, his voice a low rumble. "Learn to see what others miss. Notice the broken twig, the disturbed leaves, the tracks in the mud. These are the clues, the whispers of the forest."

Jack spent countless summers at boy scout camp, honing his skills. He learned to track animals, to read the signs of their passage – the delicate imprint of a deer's hoof, the subtle scent of a fox in the undergrowth. He practiced Kipling's old game of Kim – Keep in Memory – studying features of stones and rocks, each one unique, waiting to be deciphered and remembered. He built debris shelters in the woods, his hands roughened by the bark of trees and the damp earth.

One summer, a chilling revelation shattered his idyllic childhood. He learned that Mr. Henderson, the father of his childhood friend, Tommy, was not a businessman, as everyone believed. He was a spy, a ghost who traveled the world, his true identity a carefully guarded secret.

Jack watched, fascinated, as Mr. Henderson, always impeccably dressed, would disappear for months at a time, his explanations vague and unconvincing. Years later, he learned that Mr. Henderson had been stationed in Australia, a crucial outpost in the shadowy world of intelligence gathering.

Then there was Albert, his high school chemistry partner, and the secret he shared.

Jack discovered that his father had been a CIA agent, his family living in the heart of the Cold War, behind the Iron Curtain. He learned about the whispered conversations, the coded messages, the constant fear of being discovered. He learned how the family would turn on the shower to mask their voices during sensitive discussions, a chilling reminder of the dangers they faced.

These experiences, these fragments of hidden lives, ignited a spark within Jack. He saw the world through a different lens, a lens of shadows and secrets, of hidden agendas and unseen dangers. He felt a deep-seated need to serve, to protect his country, just as his grandfather had done, fighting in the bitter cold of the Battle of the Bulge.

He honed his observational skills, becoming a ghost in the city, moving through the crowds like a silent shadow. He would follow strangers, observing their habits, their mannerisms, their interactions with the world around them. He learned to read the subtle cues, the micro-expressions that betrayed their true emotions. He became a master of disguise, blending seamlessly into the urban landscape, a chameleon adapting to his surroundings.

The memories faded away, replaced by the grainy images of a television screen. News anchors, their faces etched with disbelief, reported a breaking story: planes had crashed into the Twin Towers in New York City. The world, as Jack knew it, had changed forever.

The phone rang, the shrill sound cutting through the chaos in his college dorm room. It was Mr. Henderson, his childhood friend's father, his voice grave but resolute.

"Jack," he said, "remember those observation games we played? The Agency is looking for young men like you. Men who can see what others miss, who can think outside the box. Are you interested?"

Jack didn't hesitate. "Yes, sir," he replied, his voice firm. "I am."

The events of that day, the horror and the ensuing chaos, had ignited a fire within him. He would use his skills, his ability to observe, to understand, to protect his country from the forces that sought to harm it. He would be a ghost, a shadow in the shadows.

The World Bank cafeteria swirled back into focus, the vibrant colors and the murmur of conversation jarring after the intensity of his memories. Jack blinked, disoriented, then quickly scanned the room, his gaze sharp. The young man from the park was nowhere to be seen.

Disappointment gnawed at him. He had lost himself in the past, allowing a crucial moment to slip away. The incident in the park, the chilling reminder of his own mortality, coupled with the flood of memories, had left him shaken. He needed to regroup, to regain his focus. He left the cafeteria, his mind racing.

He returned to Langley. He needed to delve deeper into the Chinese operation, to understand the scope of their activities, to anticipate their next move. He spent the afternoon poring over intelligence reports, his eyes scanning the pages, searching for clues, for patterns, for any indication of the Chinese agent's next move.

As the afternoon wore on, a disturbing thought crept into his mind: the car chase, the dead drop, were these isolated incidents, or were they connected? Was he being targeted because of his investigation into the Chinese operation? The possibility sent a shiver down his spine.

He took a break, walking outside the Agency towards the Potomac River, the cool evening air a welcome relief from the oppressive heat of the day. He needed to clear his head, to regain his composure.

He sat on the riverbank, the gentle lapping of the water a soothing balm to his troubled mind. He thought about his grandfather, a stoic man who had seen the worst of humanity, yet never lost his faith in the goodness of people. He thought about his parents, their unwavering support, their belief in his ability to make a difference.

He remembered his childhood, the thrill of discovery, the joy of learning, the sense of wonder at the world around him. Those early experiences, the lessons learned in the woods, had shaped him into the man he was today. They had instilled in him a deep sense of purpose, a desire to protect the values he held dear.

As he watched the sun dip below the horizon, casting long shadows across the river, Jack made a decision. He would not be intimidated, he would not be deterred. He would continue his investigation, he would uncover the truth, and he would bring the Chinese agents to justice. He would honor the legacy of those who had come before him, those who had dedicated their lives to protecting the country.

He returned to the nearby safe house to slumber, a renewed sense of determination fueling him. He would work tirelessly, he would be vigilant, he would be relentless. He would be a ghost in the shadows, a protector of the realm, and he would not fail.

The night was long, but Jack slept soundly, the weight of the day finally lifting from his shoulders. He woke early, the morning sun streaming through the window. He had a long day ahead of him, a day filled with challenges and uncertainties. But he was ready.

The next morning, Jack returned to the World Bank, this time focusing his attention on the Chinese nationals within the organization. He observed their interactions, their conversations, their movements. He noticed a subtle pattern: they often congregated in small groups, their discussions hushed, but clear.

One such group caught his attention. They were gathered in a corner of the cafeteria, their conversation punctuated by hushed tones and the occasional exchange of documents. Then the young man arrived and sat.

Jack, using his honed observational skills, positioned himself nearby, subtly eavesdropping on their conversation.

"The feasibility study for the port expansion is complete," the man stated, with a nervous demeanor.

"Excellent," replied another, a woman with a steely gaze, who Jack recognized as a senior economist at the World Bank. "This will significantly enhance maritime capabilities."

"But the logistics," a third man, interjected, "the dredging, the construction, the environmental concerns..."

"Those details will be addressed," the man assured him, a subtle hint of coercion in his voice. "China will provide the necessary resources, the expertise, the technology, if it can be funded by the Bank."

Jack's blood ran cold. He realized with a chilling certainty that these conversations were not merely about economic development. They were part of a larger, more sinister plan. The Chinese, through a combination of economic incentives, political pressure, and covert operations, were seeking to establish a dominant presence in the Pacific Ocean. They were building a network of strategically located ports and military bases, slowly but surely encroaching on American influence in the region.

Jack's mind raced. The Philippines, Guam, even Hawaii – all within reach of Chinese influence. The implications were large. The balance of power in the Pacific was shifting and the United States was losing ground.

He waited patiently, observing the group until they dispersed. Then, he raced back to Langley, his mind a whirlwind of activity. He had to inform his superiors, to warn them of the impending threat. The stakes were higher than he had ever imagined.

The air in the Situation Room was thick with tension. Jack stood before a panel of senior Agency officials, his presentation projected onto a large screen. The Deputy Director, a man whose face was etched with the weight of countless classified briefings, sat at the head of the table, his gaze fixed on Jack.

"Gentlemen," Jack began, his voice steady despite the rising tide of anxiety. "Based on my recent observations, I believe the Chinese intelligence operation is far more ambitious than we initially anticipated."

He outlined his findings: the dead drop, the courier, the World Bank cafeteria incident. He detailed the Chinese nationals' activities, their subtle influence peddling, their efforts to sway key decisions within the Bank. He then revealed the most alarming discovery: the port expansion project, a key component of China's strategic ambitions in the Pacific.

"They are seeking World Bank funding for this project," Jack explained, "using their influence within the Bank to circumvent traditional oversight mechanisms. This will allow them to expand their maritime capabilities, establish military bases, and exert control over vital shipping lanes."

A murmur of concern rippled through the room. The Deputy Director leaned forward, his eyes narrowed. "This is serious, Jack. If this project moves forward, the geopolitical implications are profound."

Jack nodded. "We need to act quickly, sir. Prevent the funding from being approved. Disrupt their operations within the Bank. Expose their agents."

The room fell silent. Then, a voice, sharp and accusatory, broke the silence. "How do you know all this, Jack? How can you be so certain of their plans?"

Jack was taken aback. "Sir, I've been monitoring their activities for months. I've observed their patterns, analyzed their interactions, and pieced together the puzzle."

"But how?" the voice pressed, "Did you have inside sources? Were you compromised?"

The accusation hung heavy in the air. Jack felt a wave of disbelief wash over him. "Compromised? Sir, I assure you, my loyalty to the Agency is unquestionable."

"Then how do you explain your intimate knowledge of their plans?" the Deputy Director inquired, his voice grave.

Jack took a deep breath, his voice steady. "Sir, this is not about 'inside sources' or 'leaks.' It's about observation, about understanding. I've spent years studying the intricacies of Washington D.C., immersing myself in the world of international diplomacy. I've learned to read between the lines, to decipher the unspoken messages, to understand the motivations of those around me. It's about being an insider, a chameleon, like the spies of old, who could move seamlessly between cultures, gaining trust and extracting information."

He paused, his gaze sweeping across the room. "We need to think outside the box, gentlemen. We need to adapt, to evolve. We can't rely on traditional methods of intelligence gathering. We need to understand the human element, the cultural nuances, the subtle power plays. We need to become masters of the game, not just players."

The room remained silent, the weight of Jack's words hanging heavy in the air. The Deputy Director, his expression unreadable, leaned back in his chair. "This is serious, Jack. We will investigate."

Jack felt a chill creep down his spine. He knew what that meant. Investigations, counter-intelligence checks, scrutiny that could jeopardize his career, even his freedom. But his concern went beyond his own fate. He feared that the Agency, bogged down by bureaucracy and internal politics, would move too slowly, allowing the Chinese to solidify their position.

As he left the Situation Room, the weight of the accusations pressing down on him, Jack knew he had a fight on his hands. He had to prove his loyalty, expose the Chinese threat, and convince the Agency to act before it was too late. The fate of the Pacific, and perhaps the world, hung in the balance.

Jack left the Situation Room feeling a chill deeper than the night air. The accusations, the skepticism in their eyes, had stung. He knew he had presented his findings with clarity, with conviction. Yet, the Agency, an organization built on trust and collaboration, had treated him like a suspect.

He needed to talk to someone, someone who would understand, someone who wouldn't dismiss his concerns. He pulled out his phone and dialed a number he hadn't used in years. The line rang once, twice, then a gravelly voice answered, "Tom."

"Tom, it's Jack," he said, his voice low. "I need to see you."

"Jack? Boy, it's been a while. What's up?"

"It's complicated. I need your advice."

"Come on down to the Tabard Inn. I'll be at the bar. Order a whiskey on the rocks. I'll be waiting."

The Tabard Inn, a historic pub nestled in the shadow of St. Matthews Cathedral was a sanctuary for weary travelers and souls. Jack found Tom in a corner booth, his weathered face etched with the lines of a life lived on the edge. He ordered a whiskey, the amber liquid a comforting presence in the dimly lit room.

"What's got you so riled up, kid?" Tom asked, his voice a low rumble.

Jack poured out his story: the car chase, the dead drop, the Chinese operation, the port expansion project, and the chilling reception he'd received at the Agency.

Tom listened intently, his eyes fixed on Jack, his expression unreadable. "You're sure about this, Jack? This isn't just a hunch?"

"I'm certain, Tom. I've seen the patterns, I've connected the dots. This is bigger than just a few rogue agents. This is a strategic play, a long-term game."

Tom nodded slowly. "Reminds me of that IMF economist case you cracked. Took a while for them to believe you then, too."

Jack sighed. "I know. But this is different. This is about the balance of power in the Pacific, about war."

"You need to corroborate your findings," Tom said. "One source is gossip, two sources is intelligence."

"I know," Jack said. "I'm thinking, there's a Canadian intelligence officer, a friend of yours from your days in Ottawa, name of Norman something. I think he might have information that could corroborate my findings."

Tom raised an eyebrow. "Norman Croft? CSIS?"

Jack nodded. "He's a good man, a sharp operator. He might have eyes on this as well."

"Worth a try," Tom said. "See if you can get in touch with him. Discreetly, of course."

They talked for hours, dissecting the situation, brainstorming strategies, discussing the best way to convince the Agency to act. Tom offered words of encouragement, reminding Jack of his resilience, his ability to see the bigger picture.

As the night wore on, the rain began to fall, a steady rhythm against the windows. The city lights blurred, casting long, eerie shadows on the streets. Jack and Tom, two veterans of the clandestine world, sat in silence for a moment, each lost in their own thoughts.

Finally, Jack rose to leave. "Thanks, Tom. I owe you one."

"Don't mention it, kid. Stay safe."

They shook hands, a silent acknowledgment of their shared history, their shared understanding of the dangers that lurked in the shadows. Jack slipped out into the rain-soaked streets, the weight of the situation heavy on his shoulders, but with a renewed sense of purpose. He had a lead, a potential ally. And he wouldn't stop until he brought the truth to light.

The morning after his meeting with Tom, Jack returned to Langley with a renewed sense of purpose. The skepticism of his superiors had stung, but it had also fueled a fire within him. He wouldn't let them bury his findings, wouldn't let bureaucracy stifle the urgency of the situation.

His first order of business was to contact Norman Croft. He found an old, encrypted email address and composed a message, carefully crafting his words to avoid detection. He recounted his findings, highlighting the port expansion project and the Chinese influence within the World Bank. He emphasized the potential geopolitical ramifications, painting a grim picture of a rising China asserting its dominance in the Pacific.

An hour later, a reply arrived, a single line in the email: "Confirmed. Corroborating evidence forthcoming."

It was from Norman Croft. Just as Tom had predicted. Jack felt a surge of relief. He now had concrete evidence, a second source to support his claims. He quickly compiled a new briefing document, including Croft's confirmation, and presented it to his superiors.

The meeting was tense. The evidence, coupled with Croft's corroboration, was undeniable. The Deputy Director, his expression grave, acknowledged the severity of the situation. "This is far more serious than we initially anticipated," he conceded. "We need to act, and we need to act decisively."

A plan was hatched. A daring, high-stakes gambit. The Agency would propose a discrete exchange of information. They would share what they knew about the Chinese operation within the World Bank, providing enough evidence to convince the Chinese to cease their activities. In return, they would demand a halt to the port expansion project and a withdrawal of their influence within the Bank.

The risk was immense. A direct confrontation with the Chinese intelligence services could have grave consequences. But the potential rewards were equally significant. It could disrupt the Chinese operation, expose their agents, and prevent a potential crisis in the Pacific.

The decision was made. Jack, his nerves a tangle of excitement and apprehension, was tasked with making the initial contact. He would use a tried-and-true method: a dead drop.

The location: Green Mount Cemetery, a historic graveyard in Baltimore, final resting place of notorious figures, including John Wilkes Booth. The message: a microdot containing the Agency's intelligence, concealed within a hollowed-out Lincoln penny. The exchange point: the headstone of John Wilkes Booth himself, a fittingly dramatic location for such a clandestine operation. The penny would be left on the first "O" in the assassin's last name.

The Chinese signaled agreement.

As the sun began to set, Jack drove north, taking a circuitous route, winding through the Virginia and Maryland countryside, his mind a whirlwind of thoughts. He replayed the meeting in his mind, the tense exchanges, the weight of responsibility on his shoulders. He thought of Norman Croft, a silent ally in this dangerous game. He thought of Tom, his mentor, his guide.

Before venturing to Baltimore, Jack decided to grab a quick bite to eat. He drove to Manneken Pis, a small Belgian restaurant in Maryland, a personal favorite. He ordered his usual: steak frites, a classic dish that always brought him comfort. As he savored the first bite, he prepared himself for the long night ahead. The game was on.

Jack arrived in Baltimore as the city lights began to twinkle. He parked his car a few blocks away from the cemetery, his heart pounding. He took a deep breath, his senses on high alert. He had a mission to accomplish, a message to deliver.

Green Mount Cemetery, a sprawling Victorian-era necropolis, loomed in the twilight. Established in 1839, it was a city within a city, a testament to Baltimore's history. Johns Hopkins was buried there, a testament to the cemetery's early prominence. King Edward VII of England was slated to be buried here for some time. Now, it held generations of Baltimoreans, their lives etched in stone.

Jack moved cautiously through the cemetery gates, the wrought iron creaking a mournful protest. The air was thick with the scent of damp earth and decaying leaves, the silence broken only by the distant murmur of the city. Rows of headstones, some ornate, some weathered, stretched into the distance, each one a silent testament to a life lived and lost.

He navigated the labyrinth of pathways, his eyes scanning the shadows, searching for any sign of surveillance. Finally, he located Booth's grave, a simple granite marker overshadowed by a towering oak. He approached the headstone, his heart pounding. He carefully placed the modified penny on the first "O" in Booth, then backed away slowly, his eyes darting around, searching for any sign of movement.

Suddenly, a sharp crack shattered the stillness of the night. Jack instinctively ducked and ran back behind a headstone, his heart hammering against his ribs. He listened intently, his ears straining for any sound of movement. Silence. Then, another shot, this time closer.

Peeking around the headstone which gave him cover, he saw the name. It was the grave of Allen Dulles, the famed former Director of the CIA, protecting him. From his vantage point, he witnessed a shadowy figure approach Booth's grave and then melt back into the darkness.

The shots, Jack realized, were just meant to scare him, to ensure the coast was clear for the other agent to quickly recover the drop. It was a bold move, a chilling reminder of the dangers he faced.

He waited a few more minutes. Then, he slipped away from the cemetery. The exchange was complete. He had made contact. Now, he had to wait.

The morning news broke the silence. "In other news," the anchor said, "the World Bank has announced it is revisiting how its funding works throughout the Asia-Pacific region to ensure it is strengthening world trade among all nations by enforcing trading agreements fairly."

Weeks had passed since the exchange at Green Mount Cemetery. There were no reprisals, no retaliations. The Chinese, it seemed, had chosen discretion over confrontation. Jack, however, remained vigilant, his senses constantly on alert. He continued his work, his focus sharpened by the near brush with danger.

Jack recessed to the solitude of the ocean beach, the salty air and the rhythmic crashing of the waves a balm to his soul. He sat in a beach chair, the warm sand beneath his feet, a sense of peace he hadn't felt in a long time washing over him. The mission, though fraught with peril, was a success.

A shadow fell over him. Jack opened his eyes to see a woman standing before him, her face framed by a wide-brimmed hat. She smiled, her eyes twinkling. "Good to see you, Jack."

MIDNIGHT SUN

The sun, a stubborn disc of fire, refused to dip below the horizon. Even at midnight, the sky above North Pole, Alaska, remained awash in an eerie, perpetual twilight. Jack Dolan, perched on the weathered deck of his aunt's remote cabin, squinted against the glare, a tumbler of icy vodka in his hand. The silence was profound, broken only by the distant howl of a wolf and the rhythmic lap of waves against the shore of the lake.

Alaska, in all its raw, untamed glory, had become his sanctuary. The vastness of the land, the untamed wilderness, mirrored the solitude he craved after the events of the recent past. The Agency, with its bureaucracy and the lingering suspicion that followed him, felt a lifetime away. He had severed all ties with time and space, disappearing from the grid, his existence reduced to a whisper on the wind.

He had temporarily chosen this remote corner of the world, this land of extremes, where the sun dared to defy the very laws of nature. Here, in the heart of the Arctic, he could reinvent himself, shed his old skin, and emerge as someone new.

He had assumed the identity of Dr. Rhys Davies, a teaching geologist based in Fairbanks specializing in geysers. The persona fit. His meticulous observation skills, honed during his years with the Agency, translated seamlessly into the meticulous study of geological formations. And the academic world, with its ivory towers and intellectual discourse, provided the perfect cover for his clandestine activities.

With hot springs and unique geology to study in Alaska, Jack's story was believable. He had studied the geysers of Yellowstone closely, the place of most geysers in the world, which he should know like the back of his hand. Iceland and far east Russia were the other places with many geysers in the world. Jack would use his cover to be able to travel through Russia to meet people on his way to the geysers.

His research was a carefully constructed facade. His true mission was to help protect US spy rings in Russia and expose Russian spy rings living in America. He needs to learn about Russians who are spying in the US by talking to contacts in Russia, to understand which US spies in Russia may be compromised by talking to Russians who want to help the Americans, and to gather intelligence on the inner workings of the Russian intelligence apparatus.

His cover as an academic should give him some liberties while in Russia. But, operating within the confines of academia, he would also be a lone wolf, vulnerable to suspicion, open to skeptics without much protection. The Russians, masters of deception, would be watching, probing, testing his loyalty. A single misstep, a misplaced word, a hint of his true identity, and his cover would be blown, his life in grave danger.

He had to tread carefully, navigating the treacherous waters of Russian society, cultivating trust while maintaining his distance, gathering information while avoiding suspicion. He would be a ghost, a shadow in the shadows, a lone wolf in the frozen north, playing a dangerous game of cat and mouse with the most sophisticated intelligence agencies in the world.

The vodka, cold and potent, did little to soothe the anxieties that gnawed at him. The memories of the recent past – the car chase, the dead drop, the chilling accusation of betrayal – still haunted him. He had survived, but the scars remained, a constant reminder of the price of his service.

He raised his glass to the fading light, a silent toast to the life he had left behind, to the man he had become. Dr. Rhys Davies, the geologist. A new identity, a new mission, a new game. And in this land of eternal twilight, where the sun never truly sets, the shadows always lurked, waiting to consume him.

He knew this was just the beginning. The game had just begun.

The air inside Langley headquarters was thick with anticipation. Jack, his heart pounding a frantic rhythm against his ribs, pushed through the revolving doors, the polished marble floor reflecting the nervous sheen of his own reflection. He had been quiet for some time, a ghost haunting the edges of the Agency's collective consciousness. Now, he was back, a prodigal son returning to the fold.

As he strode down the corridor, heads turned, whispers rippled through the crowd. He saw familiar faces, some with wary expressions, others with genuine warmth. He nodded to a few, returning the greetings with a forced smile. His gaze, however, was fixed on the balconies overlooking the atrium, where a group of senior officials stood, their faces a mixture of curiosity and guarded welcome.

He reached the end of the corridor, the eyes of the entire Agency seemingly trained on him. Then, as if on cue, a wave of applause erupted, a thunderous roar that echoed through the building. The Deputy Director stepped forward, his face creased in a welcoming smile.

"Jack," he boomed, his voice cutting through the din. "Welcome home."

Jack approached the Deputy Director, the applause gradually subsiding. "Thank you, sir," Jack replied, his voice steady despite the tremor in his hands. "It's good to be back."

The Deputy Director clapped him on the shoulder. "Your work on the Chinese expansion in the Pacific has been invaluable. Your analysis was prescient, to say the least. You've given us a crucial edge."

Jack nodded, acknowledging the praise. "Thank you, sir. But I'd like to speak with you privately, if possible."

"Of course. Let's step into my office."

In the privacy of the Deputy Director's office, Jack laid out his concerns. He spoke of the emerging threat of Russian spy rings operating within the United States, of the subtle but insidious attempts to undermine American intelligence assets within Russia. He detailed the plan: an undercover operation, a clandestine journey into the heart of Russia, guided by a trusted handler, to gather critical intelligence on both fronts.

Listening intently, the Deputy Director's expression remained grave. "This is… ambitious, Jack. Extremely ambitious."

"I understand the risks, sir. I'll be operating alone, a lone wolf in hostile territory."

"But you won't be alone," he countered, his gaze unwavering. "The Agency will be with you every step of the way. We'll provide support, whatever you need. But be careful, Jack. Tread lightly. One wrong move, and it could all come crashing down."

Jack nodded, his resolve hardening. "I understand."

They shook hands, a silent acknowledgment of shared burden, the weight of the mission, and the new renewed trust. As Jack left the office, he felt a surge of adrenaline, a mixture of fear and exhilaration. The game was afoot.

He spent the next few hours gathering his gear, a mundane task that seemed oddly surreal given the gravity of his mission. He packed light: his usual backpack filled with essential supplies, a burner phone, a few carefully selected gadgets, the geology tools of Dr. Rhys Davies, and various research papers that highlight the geysers of Yellowstone, Iceland, and Russia, a seemingly innocent compliment that would help with his cover.

Later that evening, Jack found himself at Dulles International Airport, the lights of the city twinkling in the distance. His first stop: Iceland. A brief sojourn to study the geysers, a necessary prelude to the true purpose of his journey, a perilous dance with the shadows of Russian intelligence.

The transatlantic flight was a blur of in-flight movies, tasteless airline meals, and the constant hum of the engines. Jack, however, remained alert, his mind a whirlwind of thoughts and anxieties. He reviewed his cover story and the itinerary. Every detail, every contingency, had to be meticulously planned, every move calculated.

As the plane began its descent, a poignant memory surfaced. He recalled grainy footage of President Reagan and Mikhail Gorbachev, their faces etched with a mixture of hope and trepidation, standing on the shores of Reykjavík during the historic summit in 1986. A moment of détente, a fragile bridge built across the chasm of the Cold War. Now, decades later, Jack was on the same ground, engaged in a clandestine mission that could either further thaw the icy grip of distrust or plunge the world back into the abyss of geopolitical tension.

The plane touched down at Keflavík International Airport, the wind whipping across the tarmac. Jack navigated the arrivals hall, his gaze scanning the crowd for any signs of surveillance. He found a taxi and, with a practiced nonchalance, gave the driver the address of his hotel in Reykjavík.

The city, a vibrant tapestry of colorful houses and dramatic landscapes, was a stark contrast to the sterile environment of Langley. Jack checked into the hotel, the room a cozy haven of warmth and comfort. He unpacked his bags, leaving the most sensitive equipment hidden within the false bottom of his suitcase. He took all the precautions to keep his hotel room clean from compromise from unexpected visitors while he was away. Leaving the hotel, he rented a jeep, a vehicle better suited for the rugged Icelandic terrain.

He spent the afternoon exploring the geothermal wonders of Iceland. Geysir, the geyser that gave its name to all others, erupted with a thunderous roar, a plume of scalding water shooting high into the air, reminding Jack of the mission ahead. Strokkur, the more reliable neighbor, followed suit, a mesmerizing display of nature's raw power. Jack, a geologist on a research trip, meticulously documented his observations, his camera capturing the breathtaking scenery.

As the day drew to a close, he found himself soaking in a geothermal pool, the warm water a soothing balm for his weary muscles. He reviewed his plan: a brief stopover in Moscow, a rendezvous with American Ben Hudson, a fellow geologist, from a Vermont college. Ben, unaware of Jack's true identity, would act as his unwitting accomplice, traveling with him across Russia, providing a credible alibi for their journey.

Jack knew the risks were immense. A single misstep, a misplaced glance, a suspicious question, and his cover could unravel, leaving him exposed. But he pressed on, driven by a sense of duty, a desperate need to protect his country from the encroaching shadow of Russian espionage.

Before retiring for the night, Jack meticulously checked the room for any signs of intrusion. He inspected the curtains and the furniture for hidden microphones and cameras. He slept lightly, his senses on high alert, the weight of the mission pressing down on him.

The next morning, he would begin his journey east, a lone wolf venturing into the heart of a hostile nation, a shadow player in a game of cat and mouse.

The air in Moscow hit Jack like a physical blow, a gust that seemed to seep into his very bones. Stepping off the plane, he felt a shiver crawl down his spine, a chilling reminder of the dangers that lurked beneath the surface of this city. He moved through customs with the practiced ease of a seasoned traveler, his answers to the immigration officer brief and to the point: a visiting academic, researching the unique geothermal activity in the Russian Far East. He flashed his university ID and a letter of introduction from the Russian Academy of Sciences, his carefully constructed facade holding firm.

He hailed a taxi, his gaze constantly scanning the surroundings, searching for any sign of surveillance. The city, a grim tapestry of grey concrete and austere architecture, exuded an air of brooding menace. The shadows seemed to cling to the corners of the streets, whispering secrets in the chilling wind.

He checked into his hotel, a nondescript building tucked away in a quiet side street. The room was spartan, but clean. He quickly unpacked, leaving his most sensitive equipment hidden within the false bottom of his suitcase. Then, he slipped out, his movements fluid and deliberate.

He found the bar, a dimly lit establishment frequented by locals, as instructed. He slid onto a barstool, ordering a vodka, the icy liquid burning a path down his throat. He scanned the room, his eyes finally settling on a man sitting alone in a shadowed corner, a copy of the local paper shielding his face.

Jack raised his glass in a subtle salute. The man lowered the newspaper, revealing a pair of keen, observant eyes. He nodded slightly, a silent acknowledgment.

"Everything clear at the end?" Jack asked, his voice barely above a whisper.

The man shook his head. "No issues. But be vigilant. They're watching."

Jack nodded, his gaze sweeping the room once more. The exchange was brief, efficient. He downed the vodka, a silent toast to the continued success of their operation.

He left the bar, the weight of the mission settling heavily upon him. He returned to the hotel, the anticipation of Ben's arrival a nervous tremor in his gut. The hours crawled by, each tick of the clock a hammer blow against his patience. Finally, a knock on the door.

Ben, a jovial man with a booming laugh and a shock of unruly white hair, stood in the doorway, a broad smile on his face.

"Rhys!"

Jack returned the smile, relief washing over him. "Ben. Good to see you."

And so began their journey, a perilous dance across the vast expanse of Russia, two geologists on a research expedition, Jack's true purpose hidden beneath a veneer of academic curiosity. Jack knew that the real game had just begun, a game of shadows and secrets, where trust was a fragile commodity, and the stakes could not be higher.

The Grand Express Train, a behemoth of steel and glass, pulled out of Moscow's grimy station, its departure a symphony of hissing air brakes and the rhythmic clatter of wheels on the tracks. Jack and Ben, settled into their compartment, were a study in contrasts. Ben, his face flushed with excitement, launched into a passionate discourse on the unique geological formations of the Kamchatka Peninsula, his voice a vibrant counterpoint to the rhythmic sway of the train.

Jack, outwardly attentive, listened with a practiced detachment. Ben, with his genuine enthusiasm for geology, was the perfect foil. His genuine interest in the scientific aspects of their journey would provide the perfect cover for Jack's clandestine activities.

As the hours passed, the landscape outside the window transformed into a mesmerizing blur of birch forests, shimmering lakes, and endless fields of emerald green.

The sun, a defiant orb in the sky, refused to set, casting a surreal, almost ethereal glow over the passing scenery. This was the land of the White Nights, a time of perpetual twilight when the boundaries between day and night blurred into a dreamlike haze.

After a few hours, Jack excused himself, claiming a need to stretch his legs. He strolled down the corridor, the rhythmic sway of the train lulling his senses. He reached the final carriage, a near-empty compartment with plush seats and a panoramic view of the passing scenery. He sat down, his gaze drawn to an elderly man, his face a mask of impassivity, his eyes fixed on the horizon.

Twenty minutes passed in a silence broken only by the rhythmic rumble of the train. Then, the old man, without a word, placed a small, folded piece of paper on the seat beside him and remained motionless, as if he were an integral part of the train itself. Jack, his pulse quickening, retrieved the paper. It contained a single instruction: "Hermitage Museum, 3 PM."

Jack, his heart pounding, returned to the compartment where Ben was now fast asleep, his snores a gentle counterpoint to the rhythmic clatter of the train. The sun, still hanging stubbornly in the sky, cast an eerie glow over the landscape. Jack, exhausted but exhilarated, closed his eyes, the weight of the mission settling heavily upon him. He knew that true adventure lay ahead, a dangerous game that would unfold amidst the masterpieces of art in the Hermitage Museum. He needed rest, for the shadows were lengthening, and the game was about to begin.

The sun merely dipped below the horizon before climbing back into the sky, casting a surreal, almost ethereal glow over St. Petersburg. Jack, awakened by the insistent chirping of his phone alarm, glanced at Ben, who was still fast asleep, his snores a gentle counterpoint to the rhythmic clatter of the train wheels.

"Ben," Jack whispered, nudging his friend awake. "We need to make a detour this morning."

Ben, groggily rubbing the sleep from his eyes, mumbled, "Detour? But the geysers, Rhys! We can't miss the geysers."

"Trust me on this, Ben," Jack said, his voice firm. "We need to visit the Hermitage this afternoon. It's a once-in-a-lifetime opportunity."

Ben, seeing the seriousness in Jack's eyes, reluctantly agreed. "Alright, alright. But we need to stick to the schedule. I've already planned our itinerary around those geysers."

A few hours later, they arrived at the St. Petersburg station, the city a dazzling spectacle of gilded domes and ornate palaces. They took a hydrofoil across the Neva River, the wind whipping at their faces as they approached the majestic edifice of the Hermitage Museum.

Inside, the grandeur of the place was overwhelming. They wandered through a maze of opulent halls, marveling at the masterpieces of art that adorned the walls. As they approached the Fabergé Egg exhibit, a woman bumped into Jack, her apologies profuse.

As he righted himself, Jack felt a small, folded piece of paper slip into his pocket. He discreetly retrieved it. The message was short and cryptic: "Trans-Siberian Train. Wait for Yuri."

His heart pounded. This was it. The mission had shifted gears. He needed to get to the next leg of his journey, the train east, where he would meet his next handler, Yuri.

He turned to Ben, his voice urgent. "Ben, we need to go. Now."

Ben, bewildered, protested, "But the Fabergé Eggs! We haven't even seen half of them yet!"

"Ben, this is important. We need to catch the next train east. Trust me."

Ben, seeing the urgency in Jack's eyes acquiesced. They rushed out of the museum, hailing a taxi and racing towards the train station. They arrived breathless, just as the train was pulling out of the station. With a surge of adrenaline, they scrambled aboard, finding a vacant compartment.

As the train pulled away from the platform, Jack sank into the seat, his mind reeling. The game had taken an unexpected turn. The Hermitage, a symbol of art and culture, had become a stage for a clandestine exchange, a fleeting moment of contact in the midst of a whirlwind of activity. He knew that the next leg of his journey would be even more perilous, a journey into the unknown, guided only by the cryptic message and the ever-present shadow of suspicion.

The sun refused to set, casting a perpetual twilight over the passing landscape. Jack awoke, his senses alert. He quietly slipped out of the compartment, leaving Ben to slumber. He made his way to the dining car, the rhythmic clatter of the train a constant undercurrent.

The dining car was a microcosm of Russian society. An elderly woman, her face etched with the wisdom of a thousand winters, read a fairy tale to her wide-eyed grandson. A young woman, her brow furrowed in concentration, furiously typed on her laptop, her gaze sweeping the room with an unsettling intensity. A middle-aged man, his face flushed, regaled the bartender with a passionate, albeit somewhat incoherent, monologue about the possibility of colonizing the moon.

Jack, ever vigilant, observed each passenger, cataloging their behavior, assessing their potential. The woman on the laptop, with her furtive glances and the intensity of her gaze, was a cause for concern. The grandmother, however, seemed harmless, her attention focused solely on her grandson. The man with the moon theory, while eccentric, appeared to pose no immediate threat.

Jack ordered a coffee, the warmth a welcome counterpoint to the chill of the early morning.

"Going to the moon, are we?" the man with the moon theory boomed, startling Jack. "They should've listened to me years ago. We could've built a colony by now."

Jack, trying to maintain his composure, replied, "Sounds like an ambitious project."

"Ambitious? It's inevitable! We'll conquer the stars, mark my words!" The man continued his tirade, oblivious to Jack's growing discomfort.

The bartender, a burly man with a weathered face, finally intervened. "Easy there, Boris. Let the young man enjoy his coffee."

Boris grumbled, but subsided, retreating to a nearby seat.

"He's a harmless one," the bartender said, a wry smile playing on his lips. "Boris dreams big."

"He certainly does," Jack agreed, relieved. "By the way, my name is... uh... Rhys. Rhys Davies. And you are?"

"George," the bartender replied. "Just George. These White Nights, they do strange things to a man, you know? Makes you feel like anything is possible."

"I can imagine," Jack said, glancing at his watch. "When does the dining car fully open?"

"In a few minutes," George replied, sliding a menu across the counter. "Take a look, see if anything catches your eye."

Jack thanked him, took the menu, and returned to his compartment. As he sipped his coffee and perused the menu, a strange sense of unease washed over him. He turned the menu over, and there, scribbled in pencil, were a series of seemingly random codes, names, and locations.

He realized George was Yuri and that Yuri was not a handler, but in fact, the target.

His heart pounded. This wasn't just a menu. It was a coded message, a list of names, Russian spies operating in the United States, compromised American agents within Russia, and perhaps even details of other foreign intelligence networks operating within Russia.

He quickly activated his covert communication device, a miniature satellite phone disguised as a pen. He began to transcribe the codes, his fingers flying across the keypad.

Suddenly, a knock on the compartment door.

"Mr. Davies?"

It was the woman from the dining car, the one with the laptop. "I noticed the bartender gave you a menu," she said. "Mind if I take a look?"

Jack hesitated, his mind racing. He couldn't refuse. "Of course," he stammered, handing her the menu.

She examined it closely, her gaze lingering on the back of the menu for a fraction of a second longer than necessary. Then, she returned the menu with a polite smile. "Thank you," she said, and left.

Jack watched her go, his heart pounding. Had she seen the codes? Or was it just a coincidence? He couldn't be sure.

He quickly worked on transcribing the codes. He hoped, prayed, that this information would be enough to disrupt the enemy's operations.

Ben stirred, waking from his sleep. "Hungry?" he asked, rubbing his eyes. "Let's get some breakfast."

Jack nodded, his mind still reeling from the encounter. He put the incident out of his mind, focusing on the immediate task at hand, getting breakfast with Ben. He would send the message when he knew the coast was clear.

The train continued its journey, the landscape a kaleidoscope of colors as the sun, refusing to truly set, cast a surreal glow over the passing scenery.

By mid-afternoon, they reached their destination, a small town nestled amidst rolling hills. A Russian geologist was waiting for them on the platform.

"Welcome, colleagues!" he boomed, extending a hand. "Ready to see some geysers?"

Jack asked Ben how this geologist had come to join them as their guide. Ben said he had contacted Ben a few days ago and asked to be a part once Ben shared what they were doing. Jack became suspicious. The geologist seemed to be strange for Jack's liking.

Jack, his mind still reeling from the events of the morning, forced a smile. "Ready as we'll ever be, but first I need to use the restroom."

As they boarded a fleet of jeeps for the journey to the geysers, Jack slipped away. In the secluded confines of the train station restroom, he activated his covert communication device, sending a message to Langley, transmitting the coded information.

He returned to the group, his face a mask of composure. "Ready to see some geysers?" the geologist asked again, his enthusiasm undiminished.

Jack, his heart pounding, nodded. The game had taken another unexpected turn, the lines continued to blur, the stakes seemingly higher than ever before.

The jeep lurched forward, bouncing precariously along the rugged terrain. Jack, his gaze fixed on the horizon, felt a prickle of unease. The geologist, his guide, seemed overly eager, his eyes gleaming with an unsettling intensity. Ben, oblivious to Jack's unease, was busy snapping photos of the breathtaking scenery, his camera clicking incessantly.

As they ventured deeper into the wilderness, the landscape grew more desolate. Towering mountains pierced the sky, their slopes scarred with rock fall. The air grew thinner, the silence more profound, broken only by the rhythmic thump of the jeep's engine.

Suddenly, the jeep screeched to a halt. Two men, their faces obscured by the shadows of their wide-brimmed hats, stepped out from behind a cluster of rocks, blocking their path. The geologist, his smile vanishing, raised his hands in a gesture of surrender.

"Mr. Davies," one of the men said, his voice a low growl. "We've been expecting you."

Jack's blood ran cold. He knew what this was. The jig was up.

"Who are you?" Ben demanded, his hand instinctively reaching for his camera.

The man ignored him, his eyes fixed on Jack. "We know who you are, Mr. Davies. Or should I say, Mr. Dolan?"

Jack's heart pounded against his ribs. He had been caught.

"I don't know what you're talking about," Jack said, his voice steady despite the tremor in his hands. "My name is Rhys Davies. I'm a geologist."

The man chuckled, a dry, humorless sound. "A very convincing geologist. But your act is over, Mr. Dolan."

Jack knew further denial was futile. "You're right," he conceded. "I'm not Rhys Davies. But

Ben, he's innocent. He's a real geologist. He has nothing to do with this."

The man nodded. "We understand. But you see, Mr. Dolan, your little game has put us in a difficult position."

Jack knew what was coming. "What do you want?"

"We want you to return to Washington. Now."

"And if I refuse?"

The man's eyes narrowed. "Then we will be forced to reveal certain indiscretions. Names that would be embarrassing to your country."

Jack felt a surge of anger. He had risked his life, his freedom, to protect his country. And now, they are using this information as leverage.

"You won't," Jack said, his voice firm. "I won't let you."

He knew he had to play his hand carefully. He had to find a way to neutralize the threat without compromising the mission.

"Look," Jack said, his voice calm, "this isn't going to end well for any of us. If you harm me, the names of your agents operating in the United States will be made public."

The men exchanged a glance, their faces a mixture of surprise and apprehension. Jack knew he had struck a nerve.

"We can't let that happen," one of them said.

"Then we have a deal," Jack said. "We both stand down. We both cease activities in each other's countries. We declare a mutual amnesty. All agents operating under deep cover on both sides will be declared persona non grata and expelled."

The men considered his proposal, their faces grim. It was a risky move, but it was the only way to ensure the safety of both sides.

After a tense silence, one of the men nodded. "Agreed."

Jack, relieved but shaken, returned to the jeep. Ben, still oblivious to the danger they had just faced, was busy photographing a geyser erupting with a thunderous roar.

The journey back to Moscow was a blur. Jack sat in a state of shock, his mind reeling from the encounter. He had survived, but the cost had been high.

Back in Washington, a newscaster's voice boomed from the television screen: "In other news, in a surprise announcement, the US is expelling a number of Russian diplomats living in the Washington D.C. area. The Kremlin has responded with a seemingly reciprocal measure, expelling American diplomats from Moscow. The reason for this sudden diplomatic action remains unclear."

Jack watched the news report, a grim smile playing on his lips. The game had ended, not with a bang, but with a carefully orchestrated stalemate. He had survived, but the scars remained, a constant reminder of the price of his service.

The plane touched down at Dulles International Airport, the familiar sights and sounds of Langley washing over Jack like a long-lost friend. He moved through the terminal, his movements a practiced routine, a ghost returning to the fold.

In the Deputy Director's office, Jack recounted his harrowing experience in Russia, sparing no detail. He described the encounter with the Russian agents, the tense negotiations, and the eventual agreement to expel a select number of diplomats from both countries.

The Deputy Director listened intently, his face a mask of concern. "You were in grave danger, Jack. We should have…"

"Sir," Jack interrupted, "this wasn't a failure. It was a necessary evil. We've disrupted their operations, bought ourselves some breathing room. And let's be honest, this game never truly ends."

The Deputy Director frowned. "What do you mean?"

Jack leaned forward, his gaze intense. "This isn't about ending espionage, sir. It's about managing it. About identifying threats, neutralizing some, and utilizing others."

"Utilizing others?" The Deputy Director raised an eyebrow.

"Of course," Jack said. "We have our own assets within their ranks. We gather intelligence, exploit vulnerabilities, turn their own people against them. It's a constant dance, a delicate balance."

He paused, his eyes searching the Deputy Director's face. "We need to understand that this isn't about eliminating the threat entirely. It's about maintaining an advantage, staying one step ahead. We need to know who we can trust, who we can manipulate, who we can turn."

The Deputy Director sat back in his chair, contemplating Jack's words. "A dangerous game, Jack. A very dangerous game."

"Indeed, sir," Jack replied. "But sometimes, the only way to win is to play the game."

The Deputy Director studied him for a long moment. "You've changed, Jack. You've seen things, things that have hardened you."

"Perhaps," Jack admitted. "But I've also learned. I've learned that the world is a complex place, sir. A place where morality is often a casualty, and survival is the ultimate goal."

The Deputy Director nodded slowly. "You've learned a valuable lesson, Jack. A harsh lesson, but a necessary one."

He rose from his chair. "Go home, Jack. Get some rest. You've earned it."

As Jack left the office, he felt a strange sense of detachment. The adrenaline that had fueled him throughout the mission had subsided, leaving behind a hollow emptiness. He had faced death, stared into the abyss, and emerged changed.

He knew that the game would continue, the shadows would always linger. The world of espionage, a realm of deceit and betrayal, would forever be a part of him. He had become a player in that game, a pawn in a larger, more intricate chess match, where the stakes were always high, and the consequences could be devastating.

He returned to his apartment, the city lights a shimmering canvas below. But the city, once a source of comfort, now felt alien, a cold, indifferent observer of his inner turmoil. He poured himself a drink, the icy liquid a meager solace against the chilling emptiness that had settled within him.

The news on the television reported on the diplomatic fallout, the expulsion of diplomats, the escalating tensions between the two superpowers. Jack watched the news, a detached observer, his mind replaying the events of the past few weeks, the faces of the Russian agents, the chilling threat of exposure, the desperate gamble that had saved his life.

He knew that this was just the beginning. The game had changed, the rules had been rewritten. He was no longer the same man who had left for Iceland. He had crossed a line, embraced the darkness, and there was no turning back. He was a ghost, a shadow player, forever bound to the clandestine world of espionage, a world where the lines between right and wrong blurred, and the only certainty was the ever-present threat of betrayal.

As he drifted off to sleep, the echoes of the geyser, the chilling words of the Russian agents, and the newscaster's somber report on the escalating tensions haunted his dreams. The game, he realized, never really ends.

The sun beat down on the beach, casting shimmering reflections on the turquoise water. Jack, his eyes closed, breathed deeply, the salty air filling his lungs. He had been here for a week, renting a small cabin overlooking the ocean, trying to reclaim a semblance of normalcy. But the shadows of the past continued to haunt him, the memories of the mission and the chilling realization that he was forever changed.

He opened his eyes, the sound of footsteps on the sand breaking the tranquility. A woman, her figure silhouetted against the sunset, approached him.

"Good to see you, Jack," she said, her voice a low murmur. Jack recognized it was Elena. She was a young woman who had defected to the US. She was the one who shared secrets which had tipped Jack off that it was time to go to Russia to undertake the mission.

"Elena," Jack replied, a hint of surprise in his voice. "What are you doing here?"

Elena smiled, a fleeting, almost melancholic expression. "Just enjoying the sunset. Like everyone else."

They sat in silence for a while, the sound of the waves crashing against the shore a comforting backdrop.

"It's strange," Elena said, breaking the silence. "Watching people like this. Families picnicking, children building sandcastles. It's almost alien to me."

Jack nodded in agreement. "I know what you mean. I spent so long living in the shadows, that this normalcy feels almost surreal."

"Do you ever wonder," Elena asked, her voice barely a whisper, "what it would be like to live a different life? To have a family, a home, a dog maybe?"

Jack smiled, a bittersweet expression. "Sometimes. But it's not that simple, is it?" Elena looked at him, her eyes searching. "No. It's not."

"Would you like to get dinner?" Jack asked, breaking the silence. Elena paused, then smiled. "I'd like that very much."

COINCRAFT

The biting wind of a late October afternoon whipped through Sleepy Hollow Cemetery, the ancient tombstones gleaming an eerie white against the bruised purple sky. Jack Dolan, his trench coat flapping around him like a raven's wings, navigated the maze of weathered granite, each inscription a whispered history of the past. He wasn't here for a mournful pilgrimage, however. He was here for a meeting.

Months had passed since his abrupt expulsion from Russia, a period marked by a strange limbo. The Agency, while acknowledging his contributions in Moscow, had been hesitant to fully reinstate him. The incident, accusations, lingering doubts, all cast a long shadow over his career.

To regain their trust, he had volunteered for a new assignment, a seemingly innocuous posting as an independent international economist doing work for various foundations and development organizations. The reality, however, was far more clandestine. The global financial system was in chaos, a maelstrom of volatility triggered by the collapse of several major cryptocurrencies. The fallout had been swift and devastating, rippling through traditional markets, destabilizing currencies, and threatening to plunge the world into a new era of economic uncertainty.

The Agency, recognizing the potential for exploitation, saw an opportunity. Cryptocurrencies, with their inherent anonymity and decentralized nature, provided a perfect cloak for illicit activities – money laundering, arms trafficking, and the funding of terrorist organizations. Jack, with his expertise in financial intelligence and his ability to operate in the shadows, was the ideal candidate to infiltrate this burgeoning underworld.

He had relocated to Sleepy Hollow, a quaint and storied village nestled in the Hudson Valley, a convenient base for his operations in New York City. During the day, he would immerse himself in the financial district, cultivating contacts within the burgeoning crypto ecosystem. He frequented conferences, attended seminars, and networked with traders, developers, and investors. He learned the jargon, the intricacies of blockchain technology, the allure of decentralized finance.

At night, he would disappear into the shadows, his days spent observing, analyzing, and piecing together the puzzle. He frequented dimly lit bars, frequented by traders and developers, their conversations laced with coded language and insider knowledge. He listened intently, absorbing the nuances of their conversations, the whispers of new projects, the rumors of illicit activities.

He was a ghost, a silent observer, blending seamlessly into the vibrant tapestry of the city. He was learning, adapting, becoming a chameleon, ready to infiltrate the murky depths of the crypto world and expose the hidden networks that threatened to destabilize the global financial order.

As he reached the designated meeting point, a towering mausoleum shrouded in an unnatural gloom, he reached for his phone. A single text: "Ready?"

Jack slipped his phone back into his pocket and glanced around. The cemetery was eerily silent, the only sound the mournful cry of a distant owl. He approached the mausoleum, his footsteps echoing through the stillness. As he drew closer, he noticed a figure standing in the shadows, a woman with long, flowing hair and a face obscured by a wide-brimmed hat.

"Ready when you are," she whispered, her voice a silken caress in the night.

Jack felt a shiver crawl down his spine. This was the beginning. The beginning of a dangerous game, a game where the lines between right and wrong, between friend and foe, were blurred beyond recognition. The game had just begun.

The woman, Avery, removed her hat, revealing a beautiful face etched with intelligence and awareness. Her eyes, the color of a stormy sea, held a knowing tell. "Welcome to the crypto hole, Jack," she said, her voice a low murmur.

Avery moved with a feline grace in the dusk, her movements fluid and deliberate. Her dress, a tight black number that clung to every curve, hinted at a body honed by exercise and a life of sweet indulgence. As she spoke, her voice a low, seductive purr, she would occasionally glance at Jack, a knowing sparkle in her eyes. A strand of raven hair escaped, falling across her cheek, and she would brush it back with a languid hand, her fingertips grazing the delicate skin of her neck. It was a deliberate performance, a seductive dance designed to both disarm and enthrall. Jack, despite himself, found his gaze drawn to her, his senses heightened by the intoxicating blend of danger and desire that emanated from her.

They moved away from the mausoleum. "You're right about the chaos," she began, her voice a low thrum. "The crypto crash has thrown the global financial system into disarray. But it's not just the markets that are suffering. It's the rules, the order, they're crumbling."

Avery leaned closer, her breath misting in the cold air. "You see, Jack, the beauty of crypto for these less scrupulous actors is its anonymity. They can move funds across borders with unprecedented speed and near-total secrecy. Sanctions? Laundering? Black markets? All rendered virtually obsolete."

As Avery leaned closer, the neckline of her dress dipped slightly, revealing a glimpse of soft skin. It was a deliberate move, a fleeting invitation that sent a shiver down Jack's spine. He pretended not to notice, but his peripheral vision betrayed him, his eyes drawn to the delicate curve of her collarbone, the hint of a tattoo peeking from beneath the shadow of her hair on her neck, the blended feathering of a raven. Her nipples had hardened. The air between the two crackled with a tension that had little to do with the chilling October wind.

She paused, her gaze passing over a tall, thick oak with rattling leaves that knew the secrets of the New York cemetery. "Take, for example, the 'Phantom Funds,' as we call them. They operate out of a constellation of offshore jurisdictions, leveraging a network of shell companies and crypto exchanges. They funnel money into extremist groups, funding their operations, arming their militias, all while evading detection."

Avery described a chilling scenario. A shadowy network, operating in the digital shadows, funneling millions, perhaps billions, into the coffers of extremist groups. They used a complex web of crypto wallets, decentralized exchanges, and over-the-counter trades to mask the origin of the funds. The money flowed through a labyrinth of shell companies, each transaction leaving a faint, almost imperceptible trail.

"They're using DeFi protocols," she continued, her voice laced with a chilling urgency, "to obfuscate their activities further. Lending, borrowing, staking, it's all happening on the blockchain, leaving no paper trail, no audit trail. They're building their own financial system, one beyond the reach of any government, any regulator."

Avery paused, her gaze searching Jack's. "We need to understand how they're doing it, Jack. We need to find the vulnerabilities, the weak points in this new system. And we need to do it quickly."

Jack felt a surge of adrenaline. This was bigger than he had imagined. It was a war, a silent, invisible war being waged in the digital realm. A war that threatened to destabilize the world order.

"I understand," he said, his voice firm. "I'm in."

Avery smiled, a fleeting, almost imperceptible movement. "Good. We'll meet again soon."

Avery leaned closer, her breath misting in the cold air, and as she did, her hand gently grasped his, her fingers tracing the outline of his palm. With a mischievous glint in her eyes, she slid his hand towards her, guiding it across the smooth silk of her outfit and onto the bare skin exposed adjoining her thigh. A jolt, raw and unexpected, surged through Jack. He quickly withdrew his hand. Avery had a knowing smile playing on her lips.

"In the meantime, keep your eyes and ears open. Listen to the whispers, the rumors, the undercurrents. The truth, Jack, it's always hiding in plain sight."

As Avery melted back into the shadows, Jack was left alone with his thoughts. He pulled out his phone, his fingers hovering over the contact list. He needed to inform Langley.

"Hello?" a gruff voice answered.

"Sir, it's Jack. I have a situation."

Jack explained his meeting with Avery, the chilling details of the Phantom Funds, the growing threat posed by crypto-enabled criminal networks. He emphasized the urgency of the situation.

"The world is blind, sir," he said, his voice grave. "We're operating in the dark. Countries don't understand the true flows of funds anymore. For us, spy networks are in jeopardy. Alliances are shifting, based on, well, who knows what anymore. Crypto is disrupting everything, and we're falling behind."

He described the chilling implications: the erosion of trust, the rise of rogue actors, the potential for global instability. "We need to understand this, sir. We need to regain control, or we risk losing it all."

There was a long silence on the other end of the line. Then, a single word, uttered in a low, dangerous tone: "Proceed."

Jack slipped his phone back into his pocket, his gaze sweeping across the cemetery. The ghosts of the past, it seemed, were now haunting the future. And Jack, the ghost hunter, was determined to unravel their secrets.

Jack boarded the British Airways flight to London, a touch of anxiety tightening in his stomach. The charade had begun. No longer Jack Dolan, CIA operative, he was now Dr. Jon Reed, a rising star in the world of international economics, mostly doing business as a contracted expert with foundations and international development organizations. His credentials were impeccable, forged with meticulous care. Years of research, countless academic papers, and a carefully cultivated persona had created a convincing facade.

The flight to London was a blur of in-flight entertainment and fleeting glances at the passengers, each a potential threat or a valuable asset. He arrived at Heathrow, a whirlwind of customs and immigration, before catching a connecting flight to Brussels. The Belgian capital, a city of grand squares and ornate architecture, exuded an air of understated elegance. He checked into his hotel, a discreet establishment favored by diplomats and intelligence officers, and spent the afternoon familiarizing himself with the city, the lay of the land, and the potential meeting points. He intended to meet up with old friends before the conference.

The evening brought him to a discreet bar near the embassy district. The atmosphere was hushed, the clientele a mix of diplomats, businessmen, and intelligence officers. He scanned the room, searching for the familiar faces. There, in a secluded booth, sat four men, engaged in a low-voiced conversation. Each known to one another, but each undercover for the conference the next day.

The Englishman, a man of impeccable tailoring and a stiff upper lip, introduced himself as "Sir Alistair". The Australian, a rugged figure with a mischievous glint in his eye, was introduced as "Mac." The New Zealander, a woman of quiet authority with a sharp gaze, was simply known as "Kiwi." The Canadian, a man of imposing stature with a dry comedic wit, was introduced as "Bear."

The conversation flowed easily, a carefully orchestrated dance of information sharing. They discussed the global economic crisis, the rise of populism, and the growing threat of cyber warfare. Jack offered his insights, his analysis, his concerns. He spoke of the phantom funds, of the shadowy networks operating in the crypto world, of the erosion of trust in the global financial system.

He listened intently as the others shared their own intelligence. The Brit spoke of a resurgence of Chinese influence in Africa, fueled by control of resources and trade. The Australian detailed the growing threat of Russian cyberespionage, targeting critical infrastructure and government networks. The New Zealander spoke of the rise of transnational criminal organizations, exploiting the vulnerabilities of the global supply chain. The Canadian, with a grim expression, spoke of the resurgence of extremist groups, emboldened by chaos and uncertainty.

As the evening wore on, the conversation grew more serious, more urgent. They were facing a crisis, a crisis that transcended borders, a crisis that threatened to unravel the very fabric of the global order.

Suddenly, Jack's gaze was drawn to a figure entering the bar. He stopped talking and watched. A woman, breathtakingly beautiful, walked through the door. Her dress, a sleek black number that clung to every curve of her body, was daringly cut, a slit on the side revealing a glimpse of flawlessness. As she moved, the fabric shifted, revealing a hint of bare skin beneath. Her long, raven hair cascaded down her back, framing a face that was both alluring and intimidating. The dress, designed to tease, offered a tantalizing glimpse of what lay beneath, leaving little to the imagination.

Avery.

She moved with grace, her eyes scanning the room, finally settling on Jack. A slow, predatory smile touched her lips. She approached his table, her movements fluid and deliberate.

"Dr. Reed," she purred, her voice a silken caress, "I believe we have some unfinished business."

Jack felt a jolt, a surge of adrenaline. He managed a weak smile. He was quivering.

She raised an eyebrow, her gaze sweeping over him. "Ready?"

Jack, feeling a strange mix of apprehension and anticipation, excused himself from the table. "Friends," he said, "I believe I'll retire for the evening. See you in the morning."

He followed Avery out of the bar, the cool night air a welcome relief from the closed atmosphere. "Room 1224," she murmured, her voice a silken caress against his ear as they walked towards the nearby Marriott.

The room was a sanctuary of understated luxury, bathed in the warm glow of subdued lighting. He had not planned on this, but he had to do this. He needed Avery's help. She shut the door behind them.

Avery, with a practiced grace, shed her dress, the black fabric pooling at her feet, confirming what she had not been wearing. Her body, muscular, was a marvel of athleticism and grace. She moved with a fluidity, her movements a mesmerizing dance.

The woman swayed her hips, her gaze locked on the man across the room, and with a seductive look in her eye, she glided closer, her chest shifting provocatively with each step, before she finally settled comfortably in his lap.

Inhibitions melted away, replaced by a primal urge, a desperate need for connection. Avery was a whirlwind, a force of nature, her touch both electric and comforting. Jack, lost in the moment, surrendered to the intensity of the experience, his senses overwhelmed by the blend of desire and danger.

Avery, with a playful glint in her eyes, moved deliberately guiding him inside her. A wave of pleasure washed over him. They moved in a rhythmic, sensual dance, their bodies melding together as one.

Avery whispered, her voice a sultry purr. She arched her back, her moans echoing through the room as she reached a crescendo, her body trembling.

He awoke to the sound of a gentle rain against the window. The room was empty, the lingering scent of her perfume the evidence of her presence. A note lay on the stand: "Au revoir."

Jack rose, showered, and dressed. He felt a lingering afterglow of the night's events. He made his way to the conference center, a sprawling complex that housed the summit.

The atmosphere was a potent mix of intrigue and tension. Sovereigns, their faces etched with the weight of global responsibility, exchanged guarded glances. International diplomats, their words carefully chosen, navigated the treacherous waters of international relations. And lurking amongst them, like shadows in the twilight, were the spies, their true identities concealed beneath the veneer of diplomacy.

Jack, in his role as Dr. Reed, observed the proceedings, his senses on high alert. He listened to the conversations, the whispered exchanges, the coded language. He sought out the subtle cues, the fleeting glances, the nervous tics that betrayed underlying agendas. He was a ghost, a silent observer, absorbing information, analyzing patterns, piecing together the puzzle.

The theme of the conference was "The Crypto Revolution." Speakers, ranging from renowned economists to tech entrepreneurs, debated the merits and demerits of cryptocurrencies, their impact on the global economy, and the challenges of regulation. Jack, however, was more interested in the subtext, the unspoken conversations, the hidden agendas. He sought out the whispers, the rumors, the undercurrents that hinted at the darker side of the crypto world.

One speaker, an academic from a small school, summed up crypto well, in Jack's mind, reminding of the operating consequences:

"Cryptocurrencies have the potential to empower individuals by offering them greater control over their finances and facilitating peer-to-peer transactions without intermediaries. This decentralized nature aligns with individualistic values, promoting autonomy and challenging traditional financial systems. Crypto enthusiasts often emphasize the freedom and independence that cryptocurrencies provide, allowing them to transact globally without relying on banks or government institutions.

However, the rise of cryptocurrencies also challenges the established order of international relations, particularly the principles enshrined in the Treaty of Westphalia. This treaty, signed in 1648, established the concept of sovereign states with exclusive control over their territories. In modern times, a few currencies have become reserve currencies or secondary currencies for the world, a strong positive outcome of evolution.

Cryptocurrencies, with their potential for cross-border transactions and anonymity, can undermine this system by enabling individuals and entities to operate outside the purview of national authorities. This can hinder governments' ability to monitor financial flows, enforce regulations, and combat illicit activities like money laundering and terrorist financing.

The erosion of state control over financial systems raises concerns about the potential for destabilizing effects. While cryptocurrencies can promote financial inclusion and innovation, they also pose challenges to traditional mechanisms of governance and oversight. The debate surrounding cryptocurrencies thus highlights a fundamental tension between individual liberty and the need for collective order and security in an increasingly interconnected world."

As the day progressed, a chilling realization dawned upon Jack. The world was sleepwalking into a new era of uncertainty, an era where the lines between the legal and the illicit were blurred, where the old rules no longer applied. And he, as Dr. Reed, was determined to expose the truth, to warn the world before it was too late.

The air in the conference hall was thick with the scent of expensive perfume and the nervous energy of world leaders. Jack, here as Dr. Reed, the expert economist, felt a shiver crawl down his spine. He wasn't here for the speeches, the pomp, the orchestrated displays of unity. He was here for the shadows, the whispers, the hidden agendas that lurked beneath the surface.

His gaze, however, was drawn to a figure across the room. Avery. She moved with a predatory grace, her outfit a sleek black number that clung to every curve of her body, a daring slit revealing a glimpse of flawless skin. Her long, raven hair cascaded down her back, framing a face that was both alluring and intimidating. Jack felt a strange mix of apprehension and anticipation.

He watched as she approached a group of men, their faces etched with the weight of global responsibility. She spoke, her voice a silken caress, and the men listened intently. Before parting, she gave a kiss on the cheek to one man, holding it for just a bit, and a whisper. This wasn't just a game anymore. Avery seemed to be playing dangerously.

Later, as the delegates shuffled out for a brief recess, Jack saw his opportunity. He slipped out of the main hall and into a side room, a discreet alcove with plush armchairs and a small, round table. Avery was already there, waiting.

Avery smiled, a slow, predatory curve of her lips. She removed her leather jacket, revealing the full tight black Versace ensemble that clung to every curve of her body. The plunging neckline showcased her bust and the delicate tattoo on her shoulder, a small gold belly chain accentuated her hips, and the Louboutin red-heeled boots completed the look. Jack felt a jolt, not just from the gravity of the situation, but from the raw, undeniable attraction he felt.

"The situation is far more dire than we imagined," she said, her voice a low thrum, sending shivers down his spine.

She leaned closer, her breath misting in the air. The scent of her perfume, jasmine, filled his senses. "The Russians and the Chinese, they're working together, Jack. A silent, coordinated effort to undermine the global order."

Jack felt another jolt, this time closer to his core. "Together?"

"Yes," Avery confirmed, her eyes locking with his. "They're playing a long game. They've infiltrated international organizations, subtly influencing policy, all while cultivating relationships with rogue states like North Korea and Iran."

As she spoke, Avery unconsciously brushed her hand against his arm, sending a jolt of electricity through him. He wanted to reach out, to touch her, to feel the warmth of her skin against his.

"But why?" Jack asked, his voice rough.

"Control, Jack. Control of resources, control of trade, control of the global narrative. And most importantly, control of the financial system."

Avery explained how they were manipulating the crypto markets, using a combination of official and unofficial channels. "They're creating chaos, Jack. Dumping currencies, manipulating prices, spreading misinformation. All to weaken the dollar, to destabilize the global economy."

She leaned closer, her eyes gleaming with a chilling intensity. "And they're using crypto as their weapon. It's untraceable, unregulated. They can move funds with impunity, fund their operations, destabilize governments, all without leaving a trace."

Avery took a deep breath, her chest rising and falling beneath the thin fabric of her top. Jack found himself mesmerized by the movement, his mind a whirlwind of conflicting emotions – fear, adrenaline, and a burning desire he couldn't explain.

"I have names, Jack. Names of the officials involved, the Chinese technocrats, the Russian oligarchs who are pulling the strings."

Jack felt a surge of adrenaline. This was bigger than he had ever imagined. This was a war for the soul of the global order, and he was now a pawn in this deadly game. He was close to becoming entangled with Avery, a woman who was both alluring and terrifying.

"We need to expose them," Jack said, his voice firm, though he felt a tremor of uncertainty.

Avery smiled, a fleeting, almost imperceptible movement. "We will. But for now, we need to gather more information. We need to understand their tactics, their vulnerabilities."

She leaned forward and kissed him lightly on the cheek. The contact sent a shockwave through him. He wanted to pull her closer, to deepen the kiss, to lose himself in the intoxicating scent of her.

"We'll meet again soon, Jack. Be careful."

And with that, Avery slipped away, leaving Jack alone with his thoughts. The game's stakes had never been higher.

Jack left the conference hall, his head swimming with information and suspicion. The air outside was thick with humidity of the Brussels evening, a welcome relief from the stifling atmosphere within. As he navigated the throng of delegates, his gaze swept over the crowd, searching for familiar faces, for any sign of the unseen players in this dangerous game.

Then, he saw him. A man, his face obscured by a hat and a pair of dark sunglasses, was moving through the crowd with the practiced ease of a seasoned operative. Something about him was familiar. A fleeting glimpse of a certain gait, a particular way of holding his head. But it was too brief, too fleeting to be sure.

As the man brushed past him, a small, folded piece of paper slipped into Jack's pocket. Jack felt the paper, his heart pounding. He discreetly retrieved it and unfolded it. A single line: "Mannequin Pis in one hour."

Jack glanced around, but the man had vanished into the crowd. He felt a shiver crawl down his spine. Who was this? What did it mean?

He spent the next hour in a state of heightened alert. He found a quiet cafe, ordered a coffee, and observed the comings and goings of the delegates. He kept an eye out for any suspicious activity, any sign of surveillance.

Finally, an hour later, he made his way to the Mannequin Pis, the iconic statue of a small boy urinating into a fountain. He lingered nearby, his gaze sweeping over the crowd, searching for any sign of his mysterious contact.

And then he saw him. The same man, his face still obscured, was leaning against a lamppost, seemingly lost in thought. Jack approached cautiously.

"Looking for someone?" the man asked, his voice a low growl.

Jack hesitated, then nodded. "Perhaps."

The man removed his hat and sunglasses. Jack gasped.

"Tom?"

It was his old friend, Thomas "The Gray Ghost", the legendary CIA operative who had taught him everything he knew. Tom had retired from Agency work, officially, years ago.

"Long time, Jack," Tom said, a wry smile playing on his lips.

They slipped away from the crowded square, finding a small, dimly lit bar tucked away in a side street. They settled into a booth in the back, ordering "steak and frites" and two glasses of wine.

"What brings you here, Tom?" Jack asked, his voice low.

Tom took a sip of his wine. "Let's just say I've been keeping an eye on you."

"Avery," Jack said, "I'm not sure what she is doing, but I think she is playing a dangerous game."

He proceeded to recount his work with Avery, her warnings about the Chinese and Russian alliance, and their manipulation of the crypto markets.

Tom listened intently, his expression grave. "Avery, she's a wild card, Jack. Brilliant, yes, but unpredictable. She was a rising star in the Agency, but she, well, let's just say she didn't always play by the rules. She was too ambitious, too eager to take large risks, regardless of the consequences."

He paused, his gaze fixed on Jack. "She was investigated for compromising an official that affected international markets. Her methods were not standard, to say the least."

"But you think she's still working for the Agency?" Jack asked.

"I don't know, Jack. That's the thing. We don't know who she's working for. Is she a rogue agent, a double agent, or is she truly trying to warn us?"

Tom leaned forward, his voice dropping to a conspiratorial whisper. "The Chinese and the Russians, they're playing a long game, Jack. They're undermining the dollar, destabilizing the global financial system. It could have catastrophic consequences."

Jack nodded in agreement. "For all the potential good that crypto could bring – financial inclusion, increased transparency – this, this manipulation, this chaos, it's not in our interests. It's a threat to the very foundation of the global order."

"You're right," Tom said. "We need to understand what's happening, who's behind it, and how to stop them."

He paused, his gaze searching Jack's. "Be careful, Jack. It is unclear who Avery is working for."

They finished their meal in silence, the weight of the world pressing down on their shoulders. As they parted ways, shaking hands, Jack felt a sense of unease.

He walked back to his hotel, the city lights blurring into a kaleidoscope of colors. The image of Avery, her eyes gleaming with a dangerous light, haunted him. He had to learn more about her, about her motives. And he had to find a way to stop the forces that were tearing the world apart.

Jack awoke with a start, the image of Avery's eyes, a mixture of fear and determination, seared into his memory. He had fallen asleep pondering how to approach Avery about her past, about the rumors that swirled around her time at the Agency. He needed to understand her motives, to know if she was truly an ally or a dangerous player in this intricate game.

A soft knock on the hotel door broke through his thoughts. He sat up, heart pounding. Who could it be? He glanced at the clock on the nightstand – 3:17 AM.

He slipped on a robe and cautiously approached the door. Through the peephole, he saw Avery standing there, her face pale, her eyes wide with terror. She was shaking, her shoulders trembling. He hesitated for a moment, then swung open the door.

Avery stumbled inside, her breath coming in ragged gasps. "Jack," she whispered, her voice barely audible. "They found me."

Jack pulled her inside, wrapping her in a warm blanket. "What happened?" he asked, his voice low and concerned. He poured her a glass of water, his hands trembling slightly.

Avery drank the water quickly, her eyes wide with fear. "I was surveilling them," she gasped, "the Chinese and Russian officials, the ones I told you about. I was trying to gather more information, to find out their next move."

"And?" Jack urged gently.

"They found me," she repeated, her voice barely a whisper. "They know I'm onto them. They threatened me. They said they know about my past, about indiscretions."

Jack felt a chill creep down his spine. "What did they do?"

"They said they would expose me, ruin me."

Jack looked at her, his gaze searching. "Avery, why did you do this? Why risk everything?"

Avery looked away, her face flushed. "I wanted revenge," she confessed, her voice barely a whisper. "The crypto crash, it ruined me. I started my own platform, a decentralized exchange. I thought I could make a difference, build something truly innovative. But it imploded. I lost everything – my money, my reputation."

She looked at him, her eyes filled with a mixture of anger and regret. "Those who manipulated the markets, those who profited from the chaos, they destroyed my life. I wanted revenge, Jack. I wanted to make them pay."

Jack felt sympathy for her. He understood the allure of revenge, the desire to right a wrong. But he also knew the dangers, the slippery slope it could lead to.

"But then I saw you, Jack," she continued, her voice gaining strength. "I saw your dedication, your commitment. And I realized that I could use my skills for good. I could help you stop them."

Jack felt a lump in his throat. She was using her skills honed in the shadows, to fight for something bigger than herself.

"But I moved too fast," she admitted, her voice filled with regret. "I got greedy. I wanted more information, more evidence. I compromised a Russian official."

She looked at him, her eyes filled with a mixture of shame and defiance. "I used my skills of persuasion. I seduced him."

Jack felt a wave of heat wash over him. He realized she had sacrificed her own dignity, her own self-respect, to gather intelligence. It was an act born of desperation and a desire for justice.

"And?" Jack asked gently.

Avery pulled out a small, encrypted drive from her pocket. "It worked. I got what I needed. Access to their network, their communication channels, their plans."

She showed him the data on the drive. It was a treasure trove of information: encrypted messages, financial transactions, coded communications. It painted a chilling picture of the Russian-Chinese alliance, their intricate web of influence, and their plan to destabilize the global financial system.

Jack felt a surge of adrenaline. Avery had provided them with the ammunition they needed to fight back.

He looked at her, his gaze filled with a mixture of admiration and concern. "Avery," he said, "you're in danger."

"I know," she said, her voice weary. "But I can't go back. They'll find me."

Jack knew he had to help her. "I'll get you out of here," he said. "I'll work with the Agency to make it look like you've disappeared. The Canadians will help you disappear, give you a new identity. You'll be safe."

Avery smiled, a genuine, heartfelt smile. "Thank you, Jack."

She leaned forward to kiss him on the cheek. He moved his head, and their lips touched for a moment, but he pulled away, her touch lingering. "This isn't over," she whispered. "We'll expose them."

Jack watched Avery, her figure disappearing as her clothes dropped as she walked to the shower, to rinse herself, and to start fresh. A strange mix of emotions washed over him – relief, gratitude, and a profound sense of loss. He knew that this might be the last time that he saw her. The operation to spirit her away to Canada would be swift and clandestine. She would vanish, her past erased, her identity hidden. He knew it was for her own safety, but a part of him mourned the loss of her presence. He admired her courage, her resourcefulness, her unwavering determination to fight for what she believed in. Yet, a nagging doubt lingered – were her methods justifiable? Had her thirst for revenge clouded her judgment? He couldn't ignore the lingering attraction to her, a dangerous cocktail of lust and respect. The memory of their night together, the raw intensity of their connection, still lingered in the air. He knew he should focus on the mission, on bringing down the shadowy network that threatened to destabilize the world, but the image of Avery, her eyes, continued to stalk him.

Jack turned to the new evidence, the weight of the world pressing down on his shoulders. The enemy was powerful, well-connected, and ruthless. But he had Avery's information, a powerful weapon in their arsenal. He would use it wisely, honor her sacrifice, and bring down those who sought to undermine the global order. Yet, a part of him would always wonder about Avery, about the woman who had risked everything for justice, a woman whose past was a mystery and whose future remained uncertain. He knew he would never forget her, the woman who had ignited a fire within him, a fire that burned with a dangerous intensity.

Jack returned to the conference hall that morning, a strange sense of detachment washing over him. Avery was gone, whisked away to a safehouse by a team of Canadian operatives. He felt a pang of loneliness, a strange emptiness where her vibrant presence had been. But he had a mission.

His time slot arrived. As Dr. Reed, the renowned economist, stepped onto the stage, a calm facade masking the turmoil within. He began his presentation, his voice steady, his words carefully chosen.

He described a hypothetical scenario, a chilling tale of a shadowy alliance manipulating the global financial system. "Imagine," he began, "a scenario where a coalition of actors, leveraging the anonymity and decentralized nature of cryptocurrencies, seeks to undermine the established order. They could manipulate markets, destabilize currencies, and even fund illicit activities on a massive scale."

He spoke of a "phantom network," operating in the shadows, moving vast sums of money across borders with impunity. He described how this network could exploit the vulnerabilities of the crypto ecosystem to destabilize governments, fuel geopolitical tensions, and even finance terrorism.

"This hypothetical scenario," he continued, his voice growing grave, "highlights the inherent dangers of an unregulated, decentralized financial system. It poses a serious threat to global stability, to the very foundations of international cooperation."

He paused, allowing his words to sink in. The room was silent, a hush falling over the assembled dignitaries.

"We must remember," he continued, "that the current global order, for all its imperfections, has brought us a degree of peace and prosperity unprecedented in human history. The rules-based system, the institutions of international cooperation – these are the pillars of our collective security. To abandon them in favor of a chaotic, unregulated system would be a grave mistake."

He concluded his presentation with a stark warning. "The future of our world hangs in the balance. We must choose wisely. We must choose cooperation over chaos, regulation over anarchy. The world order, with all its flaws, remains our best hope for a peaceful and prosperous future."

Jack stepped down from the stage, his heart pounding. He had planted the seed, a subtle but powerful warning.

Unknown to the audience, a silent operation was already underway. Back at his hotel, Jack had discreetly leaked the intelligence he had gathered from Avery to each of the "five eyes" spies to spread around the globe. The information was now flowing through the government offices, intelligence channels, reaching defense agencies, national security groups, ministries of finance, and central banks across the globe.

The wheels were in motion. The world was starting to wake up. Crypto may be doing more harm than good for the world.

Jack knew this was just the beginning. The fight would be long and arduous, but he had taken the first step. He had sounded the alarm, alerted the world to the impending danger. Now, it was up to the world to decide its own fate.

The sun beat down on the beach, the waves lapping gently against the shore. Jack lay back in his beach chair, a light beach read slipping from his hands as he fought sleep. He had been back in the US for a month, the events in Brussels a distant memory, though the weight of them still lingered. The world, however, seemed oblivious. The markets continued to fluctuate, the headlines filled with the usual mix of political scandals and celebrity gossip. No one seemed to notice the subtle shifts, the increased scrutiny of crypto transactions.

Jack closed his eyes, the warmth of the sun lulling him into a peaceful sleep. In his dreams, he saw flashes of the past – Avery's gaze, Tom's warnings, the tense atmosphere of the Brussels conference. He saw the faces of the world leaders, their expressions a mixture of concern and uncertainty.

He dreamed of a future where the world had averted the impending crisis, where the forces of chaos had been contained. He imagined a life beyond the shadows, a life of quiet contentment, perhaps with a partner, someone to share his life with. He pictured a small cottage by the sea, a garden overflowing with flowers, the sound of children's laughter echoing in the distance.

He wondered if that would ever come along, something that could awaken him from this solitary existence. He smiled, a wistful feel playing on his lips.

He drifted off to sleep, the sound of the waves a comforting lullaby. The world, he knew, was still a dangerous place, but he had done his part. He had sounded the alarm, alerted the world to the impending danger. Now, it was up to others to safeguard the future.

As he slept, he dreamed of a world where peace and prosperity prevailed, a world where the shadows had finally receded.

In a dream that would repeat, the air of the Canadian north bit at Jack's exposed skin as he cast his fly line into the waters of the Great Slave Lake. Yellowknife, a remote outpost on the edge of the Arctic Circle, had become a new temporary sanctuary, a place to escape the constant surveillance and the ever-present shadow of the Agency. He had taken a leave of absence, a much-needed break from the relentless pursuit of the Phantom Funds and closing the information asymmetry about crypto.

He had chosen this remote location for its solitude, the vastness of the landscape mirroring the emptiness he felt within. The days were spent battling the unforgiving elements, casting his line against the fierce current, the silence broken only by the cries of gulls and the distant howl of a wolf. The nights were spent in a cabin, the flickering flames of the fireplace casting dancing shadows on the walls, his thoughts consumed by the events of the past – the encounter with Avery, the pursuit of the Phantom Funds, the fear of his cover being discovered.

He thought of Avery. Her image lingered in his mind – the predatory grace of her movements, the intelligence in her eyes, the passion that had ignited between them. He wondered what had become of her, if she was safe, if she had found peace. He knew their encounter had been a fleeting moment of passion, a dangerous liaison in the midst of a deadly game.

While enjoying a cup of coffee at a local cafe, he spotted someone. Was it she? A woman was sitting alone at a table by the window, her gaze fixed on the bustling street outside. Her hair, shorter, framed her face, and her eyes, the color of a stormy sea, held a hint of reflection. Her figure matched his memory.

He hesitated, unsure if he should approach her. But something, a primal urge, compelled him forward. He walked towards her table, his heart pounding.

"A–?" he asked, his voice barely a whisper.

She looked up, leading with her eyes, "Yes."

HIBERNATION

The hum of the Agency was a constant, a low-grade tremor beneath the surface. Jack Dolan, his gaze fixed on the flickering monitor, navigated the labyrinth of data streams, sifting through terabytes of intercepted communications. Foreign signal intelligence, his domain now, to support knowledge of spy rings operating in DC. He had traded the adrenaline-fueled chases and the cloak-and-dagger operations for the quieter, more analytical work of monitoring and surveillance. Yet, the thrill of the hunt, the constant vigilance, still coursed through his veins.

He was the Agency's go-to expert on foreign espionage rings operating within the DC area. With over 150 countries maintaining embassies, international organizations swarming the city, and a constant influx of tourists and travelers, the potential for infiltration was immense. Jack, with his uncanny ability to connect seemingly disparate pieces of information, had become a master at identifying patterns, detecting anomalies, and anticipating threats.

He was in the midst of analyzing a series of encrypted messages originating from a suspected Russian sleeper cell when a message flashed across his screen: "Jack Dolan, report to the Deputy Director's office immediately."

A shiver ran down his spine. This was no routine summons. Something significant was afoot.

The Deputy Director's office was a stark, minimalist space, devoid of any personal touches. Jack entered, his gaze sweeping the room, searching for any clues, any indication of the gravity of the situation. The Deputy

Director, his face grim, sat behind his desk, a manila folder resting open in front of him.

"Jack," he began, his voice grave, "I need you to focus. This is not a drill." He leaned forward, his eyes intense. "We have a situation, a serious situation."

Jack braced himself. "What is it, sir?"

"A sleeper agent," the Deputy Director said, his voice low and menacing. "A deep-cover operative, decades in the making."

Jack felt a chill creep down his spine. "A sleeper agent? Here, in DC?"

"Yes," the Deputy Director confirmed. "This individual, born and raised in the United States, is the child of a high-ranking Soviet intelligence officer. They were groomed from birth, indoctrinated, trained to blend seamlessly into American society."

Jack felt a wave of disbelief wash over him. "But… how? How could they possibly remain undetected for so long?"

"Brilliant tradecraft," the Deputy Director replied. "They built a life, a career, a family. They were raising Americans, through and through. But all along, they were waiting, biding their time."

The Deputy Director paused, his gaze fixed on Jack. "And now, we believe, they have been reactivated."

Jack felt a surge of adrenaline. "What's their objective?"

"Assassination," the Deputy Director said, his voice grim. "The target is a high-level political figure, someone with significant influence on foreign policy."

Jack felt a chill creep down his spine. The stakes were high. This was a game of cat and mouse, a deadly game of shadows.

"We need to find them," Jack said, his voice firm. "We need to stop them before it's too late."

The Deputy Director nodded. "That's why I called you, Jack. You're the best we have at identifying and neutralizing these threats."

Jack felt a surge of adrenaline. This was what he lived for, the thrill of the hunt, the challenge of outmaneuvering the enemy. He was back in the game, the shadows beckoning.

He left the Deputy Director's office, his mind racing, the weight of the mission pressing down on him. He needed to find this sleeper agent, to unravel the threads of this deadly conspiracy. He had a city to scour, a web of deceit to untangle, and a life to save.

He headed towards the Italian Oven, his usual haunt. A plate of linguine vongole, his favorite, would provide some comfort, some solace before the storm. Tonight, the city would not sleep. Jack Dolan was on the hunt.

The war room at Langley was a cavernous space, usually reserved for high-level intelligence briefings and crisis simulations. Today, it was transformed into a hive of activity. Maps of the United States covered the walls, dotted with colored pins marking potential targets. Analysts hunched over computer terminals, their fingers flying across the keyboards, sifting through mountains of data. Librarians, their eyes gleaming with a mixture of excitement and apprehension, meticulously cataloged declassified documents from the Cold War era. Computer scientists, their faces illuminated by the glow of their screens, were developing sophisticated algorithms to analyze vast datasets, identifying patterns and anomalies.

Jack stood at the center of it all, a calm eye in the storm. "This is not just another investigation, team," he addressed the assembled analysts, his voice firm. "This is a battle against time. A single missed connection could have catastrophic consequences."

He outlined the mission, his voice resonating with a quiet intensity. "We are hunting a ghost, a sleeper agent, decades in the making. This individual, born and raised in America, has been indoctrinated, trained, and primed for this moment. They are the enemy within."

Jack paused, letting the gravity of the situation sink in. "Our objective is to identify this individual before they strike. We will review the files of every known Soviet intelligence officer who operated in the United States during the Cold War. We will document their lives, their families, their movements. We will trace their children, every descendant, every connection."

He gestured towards the analysts poring over the data. "We will leverage every resource at our disposal. We will utilize the latest in artificial intelligence, data mining, and predictive analytics. We will work with our partners – the FBI and friendly intelligence agencies around the world. We will leave no stone unturned."

A young analyst, her eyes wide with a mixture of fear and excitement, raised her hand. "But how do we know who to focus on? How do we identify the potential sleeper?"

Jack smiled. "That's where you come in. We need to identify patterns, anomalies. Look for individuals who have excelled in their fields, who have achieved positions of influence. Look for those who have maintained ties to their family history, those who may still harbor a connection to their parents' past."

He turned to the librarians. "We need every scrap of information we can get. Declassified files, personal correspondence, even old newspaper clippings. We need to build a comprehensive picture of these individuals, their lives, their connections."

To the computer scientists, he said, "We need to develop tools that can analyze this data, identify patterns, and predict potential targets. We need to turn this mountain of information into actionable intelligence."

Jack then spent the next few hours coordinating the effort, assigning tasks, and establishing communication channels. He contacted his old contacts, the seasoned veterans of the Cold War, seeking their insights, their expertise. He reached out to the FBI, forging a crucial alliance. He even contacted friendly intelligence agencies abroad, sharing information and seeking their assistance.

Days turned into weeks. The team worked tirelessly, sifting through mountains of data, following leads, chasing ghosts of the past. Jack, fueled by adrenaline and a sense of urgency, remained at the forefront of the operation. He reviewed every lead, analyzed every piece of information, searching for the elusive thread that would lead them to the sleeper agent. Jack often slept on a couch overnight.

Then, a breakthrough. A young analyst, armed with cutting-edge software and a deep understanding of family genealogy, presented their findings. Using a combination of public records, social media data, and ancestry databases, they had identified five families with potential links to the suspected sleeper agent.

Jack studied the list, his heart pounding. These were the children of Cold War spies, born and raised in American society, perfectly positioned to infiltrate the highest levels of government and industry. The hunt was on.

He knew this was just the beginning. The road ahead would be long and arduous, filled with dead ends and unexpected twists. But he had a team, he had resources, and he had a purpose. He would find the sleeper agent, he would stop them, and he would protect his country.

The weight of the mission settled upon him, a heavy cloak of responsibility. But Jack Dolan was a hunter, and he was ready for the hunt.

The first address on the list led them to a modest brick house in a quiet suburb of Arlington, Virginia. A neatly trimmed lawn and a porch swing swaying gently in the breeze gave the impression of an idyllic American life. Jack, along with two analysts, approached the door, their hands hovering near their concealed weapons.

The man who answered the door was tall and lanky, with a kind face framed by a shock of unruly gray hair. He introduced himself as Dr. Mark Ivanov, a soft-spoken computer scientist with a slight Russian accent that had softened over the years.

"Dr. Ivanov," Jack began, his voice firm yet polite, "we're with the CIA. We have some questions regarding your family history."

Ivanov's eyes widened, a flicker of apprehension crossing his face. "My family history? I… I don't understand."

Jack explained the situation, outlining the possibility of a long-dormant sleeper agent within their midst. He assured Ivanov that they were not accusing him of anything, merely seeking information to help them understand the past.

Ivanov invited them in, his demeanor a mixture of nervousness and a surprising degree of openness. He recounted his childhood, a childhood marked by an unusual level of secrecy and a constant sense of being different. He spoke of his parents, aloof figures who rarely spoke of their past, their lives shrouded in an air of mystery.

"When I was older," Ivanov confessed, "I discovered the truth. My parents, they weren't just scientists as they claimed. They were spies."

A long silence followed. Ivanov stared into his coffee, his eyes distant. "It was a shock, a betrayal. I felt lost, adrift. I broke all ties with them. They were gone by then, back to Russia, I assume."

He looked at Jack, a hint of bitterness in his eyes. "But you know, despite everything, I'm grateful for this country. For the opportunities, for the freedom. I built a life here, a good life. I have a wife, children, and grandchildren."

He smiled wistfully. "I became an American, through and through. I even helped develop some of the AI technology that's used in our national defense systems."

Jack felt a surge of unexpected relief. This wasn't the cold-blooded assassin they were expecting. This was a man haunted by his past, a man who had chosen the path of loyalty and service to his adopted country.

"Thank you, Dr. Ivanov," Jack said sincerely. "Your information is invaluable."

With a renewed sense of purpose, the team moved on to the next address. This time, they were met by a man named Dimitri Volkov, a boisterous individual with a booming laugh and a penchant for telling elaborate stories.

"Sleeper agents?" Volkov exclaimed, his eyes twinkling with amusement. "Brilliant idea! Imagine, generations of spies, embedded deep within the heart of the enemy! The ultimate infiltration!"

Jack and his team exchanged uneasy glances. This man seemed enthusiastic about the concept.

"My parents, God rest their souls," Volkov continued, "they were… well, let's just say they weren't exactly thrill seekers. Boring bureaucrats, the both of them. Always talking about their time in Russia, how much better things were back home."

He chuckled. "They even tried to send me back to the Motherland for college. Can you imagine? Me? In Russia? I caught the American bug, you see. Freedom, opportunity, the land of the free! I ended up at Stanford, fell in love with a Californian girl, and the rest, as they say, is history."

He gestured towards his sprawling suburban home. "Now I'm just like them, I suppose. Boring. Cutting the lawn, coaching little league, attending PTA meetings. But hey, I wouldn't trade it for the world."

Jack thanked Volkov, his mind reeling. Two potential leads, two entirely different outcomes. The search for the sleeper agent was proving to be more complex, more nuanced than he had initially anticipated.

Back at Langley, Jack sat in his office, reviewing the day's findings. Two more names crossed off the list, two more families investigated. But the elusive sleeper agent remained at large lurking in the shadows.

The next address on the list took them to a dilapidated row house in a decaying part of Baltimore. The peeling paint and boarded-up windows mirrored the despair that emanated from the man who answered the door.

He was a gaunt figure, his face etched with the lines of a life lived in excess. His eyes, bloodshot and vacant, held a haunted look. This was not the confident, successful individual they had anticipated. This was a broken man, clinging to the remnants of a life that had long since slipped away.

He introduced himself as Boris, a name that carried the weight of a thousand shattered dreams. His story was a tragic one. He had spent his childhood adrift, a ghost in his own home, constantly moving from one rented apartment to another. His parents, figures of mystery and secrecy, had instilled in him a deep-seated distrust of everyone and everything.

"They told me to learn," Boris rasped, his voice hoarse. "To learn the language, the history, the culture. To become an American. But I was always an outsider, a stranger in a strange land."

He spoke of the years of isolation, the loneliness that gnawed at him. He had tried to build a life, to find his place in the world, but the past always seemed to catch up with him. He had lost jobs, relationships, his sense of self.

"The irony," he muttered, his voice barely audible. "I was supposed to be a weapon, a tool. But I ended up a broken man, a casualty of the Cold War."

He revealed that he had indeed been aware of his parents' true identities, the weight of that knowledge crushing his spirit. Years later, he had learned a devastating truth: his parents, suspected of being double agents, had been executed upon their return to Russia. He was truly an orphan, a man without a country, without a past.

Jack felt a wave of sympathy wash over him. This was not the calculating agent they had feared. This was a victim, a man consumed by grief and despair.

"I'm sorry, Boris," Jack said softly. "I truly am."

He left the man with a sense of profound sadness. The weight of the mission, the burden of these untold stories, began to weigh heavily on him. What loyalties did these men truly owe? To the country of their birth, the country they had been forced to infiltrate, or to the fractured selves they had become?

The next few days brought a glimmer of hope. The Deputy Director informed Jack that intelligence analysts had intercepted a coded message, a fragment of a conversation, that contained a significant clue. A pet name, a term of endearment: "The Nightingale."

"The Nightingale," Jack repeated, the name echoing in his mind.

A quick search of their database yielded a match. One of the remaining individuals on the list, a renowned physicist named Dr. Andrei Petrov, had been known in his youth as "The Nightingale," a nickname given to him by his childhood friends.

Dr. Petrov. A name that sent a chill down Jack's spine. He had been living a quiet life in Gettysburg, Pennsylvania, a renowned physicist, a respected member of the academic community. A man who, on the surface, seemed as far removed from the world of espionage as anyone could imagine.

Jack and his team immediately dispatched to Gettysburg, their senses on high alert. They were closing in.

The drive to Gettysburg was a tense one. Jack, his mind racing, felt a strange sense of déjà vu. He couldn't shake the feeling that they were retracing the footsteps of history, echoing the movements of armies across this hallowed ground. Just as General Meade had pursued Lee's Army of Northern Virginia through these very roads, they were now on a hunt, a pursuit of their own enemy, a ghost lurking within the heart of America.

The farmhouse, nestled amongst rolling hills, was a picture of tranquility. A weathered porch swing swayed gently in the breeze, a garden bursting with vibrant colors. It was a scene of idyllic peace, a stark contrast to the storm brewing within Jack.

With the FBI providing security, the team approached the house cautiously. The front door was unlocked, a chilling reminder of the man's solitary existence. No one was home.

Inside, the farmhouse was a testament to a life dedicated to scholarship. Bookshelves lined the walls, overflowing with scientific journals and texts. A grand piano sat untouched in the living room, a hint of a life beyond the realm of academia.

Jack, his instincts honed by years of experience, headed straight for the study. The room was a sanctuary of knowledge, filled with the scent of old paper and the hum of a single lamp. He meticulously examined every surface, every object, searching for any sign of the man's true identity.

His gaze fell upon a book perched precariously on the top shelf. It was an old, leather-bound volume, its title embossed in Cyrillic: "Baba Yaga."

Jack, intrigued, reached for the book. To his surprise, it wasn't a book at all, but a cleverly disguised box, intricately carved to resemble an antique tome.

Inside, a trove of hidden compartments revealed a chilling collection of evidence. Microfilm reels containing coded messages, encrypted communications, and meticulously detailed reports on American political figures. There were also photographs, snapshots of a life lived in shadows – meetings with shadowy figures, clandestine exchanges in dimly lit cafes, a life far removed from the image of the reclusive scholar.

Jack felt a surge of adrenaline. They had found him.

Instead of returning to Langley, Jack made a swift decision. "We're going to Camp David," he ordered.

Camp David, the presidential retreat nestled deep within the Catoctin Mountains, was equipped with a highly secure Sensitive Compartmented Information Facility (SCIF). There, they could communicate with Langley directly, relay their findings, and coordinate the next steps without fear of interception.

With renewed urgency, Jack and his team piled into their black Suburbans and sped down the highway, the roar of their engines echoing through the valleys, their mission now clear: to apprehend the Nightingale before he could strike.

The crisp mountain air of Camp David offered a stark contrast to the tension that permeated the secure facility. Jack and his team, after a whirlwind drive, finally entered the SCIF. The room, a sterile environment of reinforced concrete and impenetrable glass, hummed with activity.

Jack connected with Langley, his voice a low growl of urgency. "We found him," he announced, his words echoing through the secure line. "Dr. Andrei Petrov. He's a sleeper agent."

He proceeded to detail their findings, describing the hidden compartment in the book, the coded messages, the photographs. On the other end of the line, analysts scrambled, sifting through the information, cross-referencing it with existing intelligence.

Back at Langley, the team with the FBI, unleashed the full force of its investigative power. Computers hummed, analyzing years of data: passport usage, credit card transactions, vehicle registrations, and even the latest facial recognition technology.

Within hours, a pattern began to emerge. Dr. Petrov, the reclusive scholar, had become surprisingly active. His usually solitary existence had been disrupted by a series of unusual movements. His plain, unremarkable sedan had been spotted in several locations, including a brief stop in Baltimore and a more extended stay in Washington D.C.

Facial recognition software, utilizing the latest AI algorithms, identified Petrov at the Washington Hilton, a renowned hotel frequented by dignitaries and world leaders. He had been staying there for the past few days.

Jack, listening to the updates from Langley, felt a jolt of adrenaline. He remembered. Tomorrow was Saturday night, the night of the annual Washington Journalists' Dinner, a high-profile event attended by the President of the United States, cabinet members, and a host of prominent figures from the world of media and politics.

"He's going to strike tomorrow night," Jack declared, his voice grim. "The Hilton. We need to be there."

The team sprang into action. Suburbans roared back to life, their engines a symphony of urgency. Communication channels were established, teams were deployed, and a silent, deadly game of cat and mouse commenced. The Nightingale was cornered, but he was still a dangerous predator.

Jack, his gaze fixed on the road ahead, knew that the next twenty-four hours would be the most crucial. The fate of the nation, perhaps even the world, hung in the balance.

The morning dawned with a heavy sense of anticipation. Jack and his team, along with a phalanx of FBI agents and Secret Service personnel, converged on the Washington Hilton. The hotel, usually a bustling hub of activity, was now a fortress, every corner meticulously scrutinized, every guest carefully vetted.

Teams fanned out across the hotel, their eyes scanning the crowds, searching for the slightest anomaly. They checked guest registries, monitored surveillance footage, and interrogated staff, but to no avail. Dr. Petrov, the elusive Nightingale, had vanished.

Hours turned into a frustrating afternoon. The initial wave of urgency had given way to a creeping sense of unease. Had they been wrong? Was this a feint, a diversionary tactic? Or was the Nightingale simply more cunning than they had anticipated?

The Secret Service, already on edge due to the high-profile nature of the event, began to express concerns. Should the dinner be canceled? Was it too risky to proceed?

Jack, exhausted and running on adrenaline, realized he hadn't eaten since breakfast. He felt a pang of hunger gnawing at his stomach. He located the hotel's kitchen, a bustling hub of activity as chefs prepared for the evening's grand feast.

As he entered, the cacophony of the kitchen – the clatter of pots and pans, the rhythmic chopping of vegetables – momentarily overwhelmed him. He scanned the room, searching for the head chef, when his gaze was drawn to a figure at the far end of the counter.

A man, his face obscured by a chef's hat, was methodically chopping broccoli. Something about his posture, the way he held the knife, the almost imperceptible tremor in his hands, struck a chord within Jack. He couldn't quite place it, but there was something familiar about him.

He focused, peering closer. The man's eyes, momentarily raised, met his. A flicker of recognition, a fleeting spark of fear, crossed the man's face. He quickly averted his gaze, continuing to chop the broccoli with exaggerated precision.

Jack felt a jolt of adrenaline. He knew, with a certainty that defied logic, that he had found him.

He slowly approached the man, his voice calm and measured, "Dr. Petrov?"

The man froze, the chef's knife in his hand. He stared at Jack, his eyes wide with a mixture of fear and disbelief.

Jack knew he couldn't afford to hesitate. He reached into his pocket, a clear shot, and he fired his gun once. The man fell to the ground, the cooking crew in total terror. The event has ended. Jack breathes a sigh of relief.

Jack, his heart pounding, holstered his weapon. He knew this wasn't over. He had to secure the scene, ensure the safety of everyone present, and prevent any further harm.

"FBI!" he barked, his voice echoing through the kitchen. "Secure the perimeter! No one leaves!"

FBI agents, alerted by the commotion, flooded the kitchen, their weapons drawn. They quickly apprehended the remaining kitchen staff, their faces pale with fear.

A cursory examination of the fallen man confirmed his identity: Dr. Andrei Petrov, the Nightingale. A small, intricately crafted vial, filled with a viscous, colorless liquid, was found in his pocket.

The investigation that followed was swift and methodical. Traces of the poison were found in several dishes destined for the main dining hall. The Nightingale, it turned out, had planned to unleash a silent, deadly plague upon the heart of American power.

The motive remained unclear. Was the target the President himself, or another high-ranking official? Was it an act of revenge, a desperate bid for recognition, or simply a twisted expression of his twisted ideology?

The evening's festivities were cancelled due to unforeseen circumstances. The Washington Journalists' Dinner, a celebration of free speech and democracy, was postponed, but not cancelled. Many believed it was the failing facilities of the Washington Hilton that had caused the event to end.

Back at Langley, Jack addressed his team, his voice weary but resolute. "This wasn't just a successful operation," he said, "it was a testament to your dedication, your skill, and your unwavering commitment to our country."

He thanked each member of the team, acknowledging their individual contributions to the mission. As he spoke, the Deputy Director entered the room, his face a flicker of admiration in his eyes.

"Jack," he said, his voice deep and resonant, "I want to personally commend you and your team. You prevented a catastrophe. You saved lives."

The praise was appreciated, but Jack felt a sense of relief wash over him. The adrenaline, the constant pressure, the weight of the world on his shoulders – it was finally over.

He was ready to return to the quiet hum of the intelligence feeds, to the more analytical work of sifting through foreign signals, for now. The thrill of the hunt, the adrenaline-fueled chases, had taken their toll. He needed time to recharge, to reconnect with the quieter aspects of his profession.

The Nightingale was gone, but the echoes of his actions would linger. Jack knew that the threat of such attacks would never truly disappear. But for now, he could finally exhale, knowing that he had done his duty, that he had protected his country from a grave danger.

Generational spies had almost worked, but Jack had helped stop it. The hunt was over. For now.

PROTOCOLS

The air hung thick with the scent of pine needles and nervous anticipation. Jack Dolan, drenched in sweat, stared at the cryptic puzzle spread across the worn wooden table. Camp Peary, the CIA's secluded training facility nestled deep within the Virginia woods, had a way of making even the most mundane tasks feel like a high-stakes operation. Today's exercise, a recreation of the Culper Ring – the first spy network established during the American Revolution – was no exception.

The puzzle, a series of seemingly random codes and historical dates, mimicked the challenges faced by George Washington and his clandestine agents. The objective: to decipher the identities of the "agents" within their training group, hidden behind a veil of assumed names.

Jack, an experienced analyst who had joined to continue to stay sharp and meet the new analysts, felt a surge of adrenaline. He meticulously examined each clue, his mind racing. Finally, a pattern emerged. The dates corresponded to significant events in American history, each linked to a famous figure. Nathan Hale, Benedict Arnold, Charlie Wilson – the names began to surface, each a piece of the puzzle falling into place.

A collective gasp erupted from the group as the final piece clicked into position. They had cracked the code. The air crackled with excitement; applause broke out.

"Well done, team," their instructor, a grizzled veteran named Agent Smith, declared, a rare smile gracing his lips.

Jack, still buzzing from the adrenaline, shared a brief anecdote. "Reminds me of a real mission I was on," he began, "I encountered a similar puzzle. I was overwhelmed, honestly. But I sent it back to Langley, and those analysts, man, they're wizards. They cracked it in record time. Unmasked a whole network of foreign agents operating in the US, even identified some compromised US assets who needed to be evacuated. Real heroes, those guys."

The team, their competitive spirit momentarily forgotten, exchanged nods of respect.

As the day drew to a close, the group packed up and headed across town to Colonial Williamsburg, a living history museum where the ghosts of the past still seemed to linger. They found a cozy tavern, its walls adorned with antique maps and the murmur of conversation filling the air. It was just a short walk from the site where the First Continental Congress had convened, a poignant reminder of the historical significance of their training exercise.

Over mugs of ale, they discussed the day's events, the camaraderie growing stronger with each passing moment. Jack, lost in the glow of the flickering candlelight, felt a sense of awe. He was a long way from his desk at Langley, but he knew that the journey continued, a journey descended from the long rich history of American espionage.

The crisp Virginia air whipped through Jack's hair as he walked into Langley. Camp Peary, with its hushed tests and academic rooms, felt a world away. Now, the familiar hum of the headquarters building, the low drone of the coffee machines, and the casual banter of colleagues brought him back to the reality of his job.

He grabbed a black coffee from the cafeteria, the bitter taste a welcome jolt to his system. He spotted Sarah, his tech whiz, hunched over her laptop, her fingers flying across the keyboard.

"Morning, Sarah," Jack greeted, sliding into the chair opposite her. "Ready to dive back in?"

Sarah looked up, a tired smile gracing her lips. "Always," she replied, "Though I could use a vacation after that last all-nighter."

Jack chuckled. "Tell me about it. But hey, at least we got through that Culper Ring exercise."

He spent the morning catching up with his team, a diverse group of analysts, linguists, and tech specialists. Each one a vital cog in the intricate machinery of intelligence gathering. He knew, more than ever, that their success hinged on their ability to work together, to leverage each other's skills and expertise.

The afternoon, however, was anything but routine. A hushed commotion began to ripple through the building, an undercurrent of unease replacing the usual workday hum. Jack, sensing the gravity of the situation, tried to gather information from his colleagues, but everyone seemed to be operating on whispers, gossip, and frantic glances.

Then, a page came through. He was summoned to a secure room, the air thick with tension. Inside, a senior official, his face grim, addressed the assembled analysts.

"We have a critical situation," he began, his voice grave. "Project Seraph, our covert operations platform, has malfunctioned. Agents across the globe are off the grid. No communication, no tracking, as if they simply vanished."

The room fell silent. Jack felt a jolt of fear. Project Seraph was the Agency's crown jewel, a system designed to be untraceable, to erase any digital footprint of its operatives. It was their lifeline, their insurance policy. If it had failed, it meant that agents were exposed, their identities compromised, their very existence erased from the Agency's records.

"We don't know what caused this," the official continued, "but we need to find out, and fast. This could have catastrophic consequences. Lives are at stake."

Jack, his mind reeling, realized the gravity of the situation. Project Seraph was more than just a piece of technology; it was the foundation upon which their entire operation rested. And now, that foundation was crumbling, threatening to bury them all.

He knew this was just the beginning. The hunt for the truth had just begun, and the stakes couldn't be higher.

Jack gathered his team, a motley crew of computer wizards who could dissect a firewall with a single line of code. Sarah, his tech whiz, was there, of course, along with Ben, the network guru, and Anya, the encryption expert.

"Alright, team," Jack began, the gravity of the situation heavy in the air. "We need to understand how this happened. Project Seraph – it's the heart of everything we do. Who's where, when, under what cover, mission parameters, even family details for emergency contacts – it's all in there. Gone are the days of dusty files. This system was supposed to be impenetrable."

Ben, his brow furrowed, chimed in, "It was. Redundant systems, triple-layered encryption, constant monitoring, it should have been impossible to bring it down."

"So, what happened?" Jack pressed.

Anya, her eyes fixed on the screen, explained, "Project Seraph isn't entirely housed within Langley. We utilize cloud technology, the most advanced the private sector offers. Rigorously vetted companies, top-tier security, but…"

"But someone got in," Sarah finished, her voice grim. "Compromised the third-party provider, the entry point for the entire system."

Jack felt a chill crawl down his spine. "Who? And how?"

The team fell silent, each lost in their own thoughts. Ben started typing furiously, his fingers a blur on the keyboard.

"I'm pulling up the intrusion logs," he muttered, "trying to trace the attack vector. It's sophisticated, highly targeted. Whoever did this knew exactly what they were doing."

Hours turned into the late night. The team worked tirelessly, dissecting the attack, piecing together the puzzle. The picture that emerged was terrifying. The third-party provider, a company renowned for its cybersecurity, had been breached by a highly skilled adversary. The attack was subtle, insidious, designed to remain undetected for as long as possible.

"They infiltrated the system months ago," Anya said, her voice grave. "Slowly, meticulously, they gained access to core components, planting backdoors, manipulating data streams."

"And now," Ben added, "they've crippled Seraph, leaving us blind, vulnerable."

The weight of their findings settled heavily on the team. Project Seraph was down, and their agents were out there, operating in the shadows, completely cut off from their support network. The enemy had gained a significant advantage, and the consequences could be devastating.

Jack knew this was only the beginning. They had to find a way to restore Seraph, to regain control, and to hunt down the entity responsible for this attack. The fate of countless lives, and the very fabric of their organization, now hung in the balance.

The pressure was immense. Jack's team, these brilliant minds, the best of the best, were under intense scrutiny. They were the invisible warriors, their work just as critical as the spies operating in the shadows. They were the future, the cutting edge of intelligence gathering in the digital age.

"We rely on these third-party providers," Ben explained, pacing in front of the whiteboard where a complex network diagram was slowly taking shape. "Specialization is key. They're experts in their fields, cloud computing, AI, quantum encryption – areas where we simply can't compete internally. It's more efficient, more cost-effective."

"But it also creates vulnerabilities," Sarah pointed out, her eyes glued to the screen. "Single points of failure."

The team spent the next few days meticulously tracing the attack. They analyzed network traffic, decoded encrypted messages, and pieced together the puzzle like forensic archaeologists. The trail led them to a cluster of servers in Eastern Europe, a region known for its shadowy cybercriminal organizations.

"It appears to be a rogue group," Anya concluded, her voice grave. "Highly organized, well-funded. They're not your typical script kiddies. This was a sophisticated operation, months in the making."

The weight of their findings settled heavily on Jack. This wasn't just a technical issue; it was a declaration of war. Someone was trying to cripple the Agency, to blindside them, to dismantle their ability to operate effectively.

With the preliminary findings in hand, Jack sought an audience with the Deputy Director, a seasoned veteran with a steely gaze and a reputation for decisive action.

"Deputy Director," Jack began, his voice firm, "Project Seraph is compromised. We believe the attack originated from Eastern

Europe, a highly sophisticated operation targeting the third-party provider."

The Deputy Director leaned forward, his expression grave. "The implications are severe."

"Yes, sir. Agents are off the grid. We're blind, vulnerable. This could have catastrophic consequences."

He considered this for a moment, his eyes scanning the room. "We need to contain this. Isolate the breach, restore communications with our assets. And we need to find out who is behind this."

"We're already working on it, sir. But we need resources and the authority to engage with our international partners."

He nodded. "Consider it done. This is a top priority. I want updates, Jack. I want to know everything."

Leaving the office, Jack felt a renewed sense of purpose. The stakes had never been higher. The enemy was out there, lurking in the shadows, and they were determined to bring the Agency to its knees. But Jack and his team wouldn't back down. They would fight back, they would hunt down the culprits, and they would restore Project Seraph, piece by agonizing piece. The fate of the Agency, and perhaps the nation itself, now rested on their shoulders.

The clock was ticking. Every minute that Seraph remained offline was a risk, a vulnerability. Jack's team, fueled by adrenaline and a fierce sense of urgency, worked tirelessly. They collaborated with the third-party providers, their engineers forming a symbiotic unit.

The first step was containment. The breach, a cunning exploit that had leveraged a zero-day vulnerability in the provider's network, had to be isolated. Firewalls were erected, traffic was rerouted, and infected systems were quarantined. It was like battling a digital wildfire, containing the flames before they could consume the entire forest.

Next came the restoration. The team focused on rebuilding critical pathways, establishing secure tunnels between Langley and the provider's network. Stateless servers, designed to minimize the impact of compromised systems, were deployed, creating a more resilient infrastructure. Redundancy was key – multiple connections, diverse routes, and fail-safe mechanisms were implemented to ensure uninterrupted communication.

The process was painstaking, a delicate dance of code and countermeasures. They meticulously analyzed the attack logs, identifying the adversary's tactics, their methods of infiltration. They learned from their mistakes, hardening the system against future attacks, implementing multi-factor authentication, and enhancing encryption protocols.

Days turned into nights, fueled by caffeine and a shared determination. The team, pushed to their limits, found a renewed sense of purpose. They were not just fixing a system; they were defending the very heart of the Agency, safeguarding the lives of their colleagues.

Finally, after what felt like an eternity, the first glimmer of success. A critical communication channel was re-established. A ping, a faint echo across the digital void, confirming that contact had been restored.

The team erupted in cheers, the tension that had gripped them for days finally releasing. One by one, the systems began to come back online. The flow of information, the lifeblood of the Agency, started to trickle, then gush, back into the system. Seraph was breathing again.

News of their success spread through the Agency like wildfire. Relief washed over Jack and his team, a profound sense of accomplishment. They had stared into the abyss, faced an unseen enemy, and emerged victorious.

The Deputy Director appeared in their workspace, a rare smile gracing his lips. "Colleagues," he said, his voice filled with admiration, "you have saved the day. The Agency owes you a debt of gratitude."

Jack, humbled by the praise, knew that this was just the beginning. The threat landscape was constantly evolving, and the enemy would undoubtedly return. But they were ready. They had learned, they had adapted, and they were stronger. The battle for the digital frontier had just begun.

The immediate crisis had passed. Seraph was back online, communication with agents restored, and the initial wave of panic had subsided. Jack found himself in the Deputy Director's office, a more relaxed atmosphere than their previous meeting.

"You and your team," he began, "you were instrumental. You averted a disaster."

"We were fortunate, sir," Jack replied, "The team worked tirelessly. They're the real heroes."

"Humility is a virtue, Jack, but I've seen the reports. You provided crucial leadership, kept the team focused, and made some key decisions that undoubtedly accelerated our recovery."

Jack nodded, acknowledging the praise. "We were able to quickly isolate the breach and establish alternate pathways," he explained, "and we implemented several countermeasures to prevent the adversary from exploiting the same vulnerabilities."

"But you've also discovered something else, haven't you?" he inquired, his gaze sharp.

Jack hesitated, then nodded. "There's a possibility, sir, that the attack, while originating from Eastern Europe, may have deeper roots. Potential funding sources in the Middle East. Retaliation, perhaps, for some of the cyber operations we've assisted our allies with in the region."

The Deputy Director leaned back in his chair, pondering the implications. "A long game, then. They're not just trying to disrupt our operations; they're trying to send a message."

"It's a possibility, sir. But we still have the best and brightest in this building, and at the NSA. We'll stay ahead of them."

The Deputy Director nodded approvingly. "I have no doubt. You and your team have proven that. Now, get some rest. You've earned it."

As Jack left the office, he couldn't shake the feeling that this was just the beginning of a new era of cyber warfare, a shadow war fought in the unseen realms of the digital world.

The enemy was out there, relentless and determined. But so were they. The Agency, with its dedicated teams of analysts, engineers, and operatives, would continue to defend the nation, one line of code, one intercepted message, one thwarted attack at a time.

CIPHER

•

The sunrise, a fiery kiss across the Potomac, painted the sky in hues of orange and pink. Jack Dolan, a veteran of the Agency, traded in his old apartment for a cozy rowhouse in Alexandria, a stone's throw from where George Washington himself once roamed. He'd earned it. After years of relentless pursuit, of chasing shadows and deciphering whispers, he was now Chief of the Immediate Office for Surveillance of Foreign Spy Rings, a fancy title for the team that had become his second family.

He had climbed the ranks, not by backstabbing colleagues or currying favor with superiors, but by proving himself. He understood the analysts, knew their frustrations, their triumphs. He had been there, hunched over terminals, staring at blinking cursors, deciphering cryptic messages, the weight of the nation resting on his shoulders. He was their advocate, their leader, a bridge between the boots on the ground and the suits in the boardrooms.

The morning commute became a ritual. A black sedan, discreet and unmarked, whisked him up the river, the familiar landmarks flashing by – the Pentagon, the Lincoln Memorial, a constant reminder of the weight of his responsibilities. He entered Langley, the familiar hum of the Agency washing over him, a low-grade tremor beneath the surface. The scent of old coffee and stale air hung heavy in the hallways, a comforting familiarity.

His office, a spacious corner room with panoramic views of the Virginia countryside, was a testament to his success. Yet, it felt more like a command center than a personal space. Maps adorned the walls, a constant reminder of the global chessboard, each pin representing a potential threat.

The day unfolded in a whirlwind of briefings, intelligence reports, and urgent phone calls. He reviewed surveillance logs, analyzed intercepted communications, and coordinated with other agencies, his voice a calm counterpoint to the frenetic energy that permeated the office.

As the sun began to set, casting long shadows across the Virginia landscape, Jack decided to take a break. He headed towards the waterfront in Old Town Alexandria, the city lights twinkling in the distance. He found a spot on the pier, the cool evening breeze a welcome respite from the stifling heat of the day.

A tall ship replica, its sails furled, dominated the harbor. As the sky erupted in a kaleidoscope of colors, a symphony of fireworks painting the night sky, Jack felt a sense of peace descend upon him. He had come a long way, from a rookie analyst to the Chief, leading the fight against unseen enemies. But amidst the chaos, amidst the constant vigilance, he had found a measure of tranquility, a quiet appreciation for the beauty of the world he was sworn to protect.

The fireworks continued, a dazzling display of light and sound, a celebration of freedom and resilience. It was July 3rd, and some were practicing a day ahead. Jack watched, a small smile playing on his lips. He had a long road ahead, a constant battle against the shadows, but for this fleeting moment, he allowed himself to simply enjoy the spectacle, to savor the quiet joy of a job well done.

The air hung heavy, thick with the scent of barbeque and the promise of fireworks. It was the Fourth of July, a day for celebration, a day for reflection. Jack, however, found himself strangely unsettled. The usual patriotic fervor felt muted, replaced by a lingering unease. Maybe it was the weight of the world, the constant threat of unseen enemies, the ever-present shadow of global instability.

He was about to test the grill for later, the aroma of sizzling burgers and hot dogs already tantalizing his senses, when his phone buzzed. It was a text from an unexpected source: Marcus "Mac" Reilly, his gruff old instructor from Camp Peary, the CIA's infamous training facility.

"Jack," the text read, "need your eye. Something's brewing in Williamsburg. Strange message. Meet me when you can."

Mac Reilly was no stranger to the bizarre. A legend in the Agency, he'd seen and done it all, from deep-cover operations in the heart of the Soviet Union to extracting assets from hostile territory. If he was intrigued, Jack knew it was serious.

The idea of a road trip on the Fourth of July wasn't exactly appealing, but the prospect of unraveling a mystery, especially one involving Mac Reilly, was too tempting to resist. He quickly packed a bag, grabbed a cooler stocked with cold drinks, and hit the road.

The drive to Williamsburg was a pleasant one, the summer sun glinting off the highway. Mac Reilly's house was a quaint colonial, nestled amongst the mature trees of a quiet neighborhood. He greeted Jack with a gruff smile and a bottle of bourbon. "Welcome, Jack. Glad you could make it."

"What's this all about, Mac?" Jack inquired, taking a long sip of the bourbon. "Some kind of historical conspiracy?"

Mac chuckled, "You could say that. It involves an art curator, a friend of mine. She was cleaning a portrait of Governor Fauquier, you know, the one hanging in the Governor's Palace. On the back, she found something unusual."

He led Jack to his study, a room overflowing with books and antique maps. On the desk lay a framed photograph of the Governor's Palace portrait. "This is it," Mac said, pointing to a barely visible inscription on the back.

Jack leaned closer, squinting at the faded text. It seemed to be some kind of coded message, a series of cryptic phrases seemingly referencing George Washington.

"What do you make of it?" Mac asked, his eyes twinkling with anticipation.

Jack studied the inscription, his brow furrowed. "It's... intriguing. But I can't quite decipher it. It feels like a puzzle, a riddle with a missing piece."

"That's what I thought," Mac agreed. "But I believe there's more to it. This isn't just some idle speculation. Someone, somewhere, is trying to tell us something."

"We need to find out what," Jack said, a spark of excitement igniting within him. "This could be interesting, Mac."

"Indeed," Mac replied, a mischievous glint in his eye. "Let's head to Chowning's Tavern. We can exchange stories, enjoy a proper Virginia meal, and try to make some sense of this."

As they traveled towards Colonial Williamsburg, the sounds of revelry filled the air. Children chased fireflies, the aroma of roasting pig filled the air, and the strains of patriotic music drifted from a nearby tavern. The Fourth of July was a special time, a celebration of independence, but also now, perhaps the beginning of a new hunt, a quest to uncover a long-buried secret, a secret that could rewrite the very foundations of American history.

Jack awoke to the sound of birdsong filtering through the open window. The morning sun, already high in the sky, cast long shadows across the room. He stretched, a crick in his neck a testament to the late hours spent poring over the cryptic message. Mac Reilly, bless his soul, had insisted on a nightcap, and the conversation had flowed like the finest Virginia wine.

Today, the hunt was on.

Jack showered and dressed, the faded inscription on the back of the Governor's Palace portrait still dancing in his mind. George Washington. The Father of his Country. A man shrouded in myth and legend. But what if the legends weren't just legends? What if there was a hidden truth, a secret history waiting to be unearthed?

Jack spent the morning immersed in research. He devoured biographies, historical accounts, and even delved into the murky world of conspiracy theories. He learned about the enduring myths surrounding Washington: the "I cannot tell a lie" cherry tree incident, the "silver dollar thrown across the Rappahannock", the superhuman strength, the almost mythical aura that clung to him.

He meticulously examined Washington's early life. Born in 1732 at the family plantation, the narrative was straightforward. Yet, discrepancies emerged. The exact date of his birth was shrouded in some ambiguity. Some accounts placed it on February 11th, others on February 22nd. Minor discrepancies, perhaps, but to Jack, they were intriguing.

He delved into the historical context. The 18th century was a time of flux, a period of great social and political upheaval. The colonies were grappling with their identity, yearning for independence from British rule. In such a volatile climate, information could be manipulated, truths could be obscured.

As he delved deeper, a chilling thought emerged. What if Washington's origins were deliberately obscured? What if there was a reason to conceal the truth about his birth, a reason so powerful that it necessitated the creation of a carefully crafted myth?

Jack felt a shiver crawl down his spine. This wasn't just a historical curiosity; it was a potential threat, a dangerous secret that could destabilize the very foundations of the nation.

He met Mac Reilly at a coffeeshop in Colonial Williamsburg, the aroma of freshly brewed coffee filling the air, a place to talk.

"Any luck?" Mac asked, his eyes twinkling.

Jack recounted his findings, focusing on the inconsistencies surrounding Washington's birth date and the growing sense of unease that had settled over him.

Mac listened intently, his brow furrowed. "You know," he mused, "there are whispers, old wives' tales, about Washington's birth."

Jack leaned forward, intrigued. "What kind of stories?"

Mac hesitated, a wary look in his eyes. "Just rumors, Jack. But sometimes, the most outlandish rumors have a grain of truth buried within them."

He paused, taking a sip of his coffee. "We need to dig deeper. Explore the archives, interview historians, uncover any hidden records."

Jack felt a surge of adrenaline. This was exactly the kind of challenge he craved. A puzzle to solve, a conspiracy to unravel. He was ready to dive headfirst into the murky waters of history, to uncover the truth, no matter where it led.

Jack spent the next few days immersed in research, a whirlwind of dusty archives, forgotten journals, and faded letters. He meticulously pieced together Mary Ball Washington's life, tracing her movements through old land records and social registers.

The more he delved, the more intrigued he became. Mary, a woman of considerable social standing, had been quite the social butterfly. Her father, a prominent figure in Virginia society, had served as a Burgess in the House of Burgesses. Jack discovered that Mary had maintained close ties with her father's friends and associates, even after his death.

One particular entry in the social register caught his eye. In 1732, Mary had undertaken a journey to Williamsburg, the colonial capital. She had stayed with a close friend of her father's, a wealthy merchant with connections to the Royal Governor. The timing was uncanny.

A chill ran down Jack's spine. Was it possible? Could George Washington have been born not at his family's plantation on Popes Creek in Westmoreland County, Virginia, but in the heart of colonial power, within the very walls of Williamsburg?

The implications were interesting. If true, it would change the carefully constructed myth of the humble Virginia planter. If proven untrue, it would raise more questions about his lineage, his connections, and the very foundation of his identity.

But why? Why would such a seemingly innocuous detail be concealed? What was the nature of the conspiracy, and who would benefit from it?

Jack returned to the Governor's Palace portrait, the cryptic message on the back taunting him. He spent hours staring at the inscription, trying to decipher the hidden meaning. He played with the letters, rearranged them, searched for hidden codes, anagrams, anything that might unlock the puzzle.

Then, it hit him. A simple, almost childish pattern. The letters, when read in a specific order, formed a sentence.

"George Washington was born in 1732 in Williamsburg at the Royal Governor's Palace."

A wave of dizziness washed over him. Had he actually cracked the code? Was it really that simple?

But was it true? Was there any truth to this seemingly outlandish claim? Why would anyone go to such lengths to conceal such a seemingly trivial detail?

Jack took a deep breath, the weight of the discovery settling upon him. He had a long way to go. He needed to check it again, to understand the implications of this startling revelation.

Jack took another deep breath, the air thick with the weight of history, the scent of ancient secrets. He had stumbled upon something extraordinary, something that could rewrite history and the very narrative of the greatest founding father. The question now was, what did it all mean?

Jack felt a newfound freshness to the problem. He poured out his discovery, the deciphered message, the intriguing details about Mary Ball Washington's trip to Williamsburg.

Mac listened intently, his eyes widening with each revelation. "If this is true," he breathed, "it changes everything."

"I know," Jack said, his voice low. "But why? Why would they go to such lengths to conceal it?"

A long silence followed. They pondered the implications. Was it simply a matter of preserving Washington's image as a humble Virginia planter? Or was there something more deeper, more insidious reason for the cover-up?

"Could it be something more than just image?" Mac mused. "What if there was a political motive? What if his birth within the confines of the Royal Governor's Palace somehow compromised his claim to the presidency?"

Jack's eyes widened. "Compromised his claim? How?"

Mac leaned forward, his voice dropping to a conspiratorial whisper. "Think about it, Jack. If George Washington was truly born within the walls of the Royal Governor's Palace, wouldn't that make him, in a sense, born on British soil?"

Jack stared at him, the implications sinking in. "You mean… like, he was born in an embassy of a foreign country... he wouldn't be a natural-born citizen?"

"Exactly," Mac said, his voice grave. "The Constitution clearly states that the President must be a natural-born citizen. Born in the United States. If Washington was born within the confines of the Royal Governor's Palace, a symbol of British authority and sovereignty, wouldn't that technically make him British by soil?"

A chilling silence descended upon them. The implications were staggering. If Washington was not a natural-born citizen, his entire presidency would be illegitimate.

"Like Hamilton," Jack said, his voice trembling. "Alexander Hamilton, born in the West Indies, was ineligible for the presidency. Different, in so far as, St. Kitts and Nevis never became an American territory, but similar, as Hamilton was not a natural-born citizen. This could invalidate Washington's entire legacy."

Mac nodded solemnly. "It would throw the very foundations of this nation into question. The first president, the Father of his Country, an imposter and illegitimate from the start."

The weight of their discovery pressed down on them. The implications were profound, far-reaching, and potentially devastating.

Mac, sensing Jack's distress, poured him a generous shot of Virginia whiskey. "To discovering the truth," he said, raising his glass.

Jack took a long sip, the fiery liquid burning a path down his throat. The truth, he realized, might be more unbelievable than they could have ever imagined.

The weight of their discovery hung heavy in the air, a suffocating blanket of disbelief and dread. Jack and Mac sat in stunned silence, the implications of their findings echoing in the quiet room.

"We can't let this out," Mac finally said, his voice hoarse. "Not now. Not ever."

Jack nodded, his mind reeling. The repercussions of revealing Washington's "true" birthplace would be catastrophic. It would tear at the fabric of American history, throw the nation into a constitutional crisis, and potentially ignite a firestorm of political and social unrest.

"The big anniversary of American independence is coming up," Jack said, his voice grim. "We can't risk destabilizing the country, not now."

"Agreed," Mac said. "We need to bury this secret. Deep."

They spent the next hour debating the best course of action. In the end, they decided to return to the art curator and they would tell her that the inscription was nothing more than a fanciful inscription, perhaps a personal note from the artist, a whimsical flourish with no real significance. They would assure her that it was best left undisturbed, a forgotten curiosity buried within the folds of history.

With a heavy heart, Mac contacted the curator. He explained their findings, emphasizing the likely inconsequential nature of the inscription. The curator, relieved, agreed to keep the matter confidential.

As they walked in Colonial Williamsburg, a strange sense of unease settled over them. They had stumbled upon a truth so profound, so potentially destabilizing, that they had chosen to bury it. They had become keepers of a secret, custodians of a hidden history.

"We can't tell anyone about this, Mac," Jack said, his voice grave. "Not ever."

Mac nodded solemnly. "This goes to the grave with us, Jack. We can't let this poison the well of American history."

They shared a long, silent look, the weight of their unspoken pact hanging heavy between them. They had faced down enemies foreign and domestic, navigated treacherous political landscapes, and confronted the darkest corners of the human soul. But this, this was different. This was a secret that had to remain buried, a truth too strange to be unleashed upon the world.

As they walked to the tavern into the fading light, Jack couldn't shake the feeling that they had made a Faustian bargain. They had saved the nation from a potential constitutional crisis, but at the cost of the truth. The truth, a powerful force, had been silenced.

In silence, the two carried the weight of their shared secret, a heavy burden, a constant reminder of the price of protecting the myth.

HIGHWATER

The salty air whipped through Jack Dolan's hair as he squinted at the horizon. The sun, a malevolent eye in the cerulean sky, beat down on the sand, baking the grains into a shimmering expanse. Key West, a vibrant island of escape, felt a million miles away from the sterile corridors of Langley. Yet, the weight of the world, of the ever-shifting geopolitical chessboard, seemed to follow him even here.

He closed his eyes, the rhythmic crash of the waves against the shore a lullaby against the intrusive thoughts. The ghost of past missions haunted him – the car chase, the expulsion from Moscow, the encounter with Avery, and the sleeper agent coming alive. Each operation, a victory hard-won, a reminder of the constant vigilance required to protect the nation.

But the world, it seemed, was always one step ahead. New threats emerged daily, more insidious, more elusive. Cyberattacks, orchestrated from anonymous corners of the globe, crippled critical infrastructure. Disinformation campaigns, weaponized with surgical precision, eroded trust and sowed discord. And the old adversaries, like resilient weeds, continued to sprout, adapting, evolving.

Could they keep up? Could he, his team, with their resources and budget, truly stay ahead of the curve? The question gnawed at him, a persistent itch beneath the surface of his relaxation.

He opened his eyes, the vibrant colors of the beach assaulting his senses. Turquoise water, white sand, the lazy sway of a few palm trees. He needed this. A chance to recharge, to let the weight of the world melt away, even if only for a few precious days. He focused on the simple pleasures: the warmth of the sun on his skin, the taste of the margarita he'd sipped earlier, the playful calls of the seagulls.

He pulled his sunglasses down, the glare of the sun momentarily blinding him. A text message pinged on his phone. He squinted at the screen:

Langley: Are you in Key West?

A frown creased his brow. How did they know? He quickly typed his reply:

Jack: Yes.

Another text arrived almost instantly:

Langley: Find a secure phone and call in. There is a situation that needs your attention.

The weight of the world, it seemed, had found him even here. Jack sighed, the idyllic tranquility shattered. He packed up his beach gear, the playful mood replaced by a grim determination. He had a feeling this "situation" wouldn't wait. He headed back to the

Weatherstation Inn, the irony of its name not lost on him. The weather, it seemed, was always changing. And so were the threats.

Jack slid into the worn leather armchair in his hotel room, the secure phone cradled between his ear and shoulder. The air-conditioning hummed, a feeble counterpoint to the rising panic within him. His vacation, barely begun, had already been torpedoed.

"Jack," the voice on the other end was clipped, businesslike, "we have a situation. A heist. Occurred earlier this evening at the Mel Fisher Maritime Museum."

Jack's eyebrows shot up. "The Mel Fisher? The one with the Atocha treasure?"

"Precisely. A single item was taken – the 'Sunken Idol,' a pre-Columbian artifact believed to be linked to a cache of Spanish gold rumored to have been lost at sea."

"A heist? Why is the CIA involved?" Jack's voice was sharp.

"National security, Jack. This isn't just about a priceless artifact. Intelligence suggests multiple foreign actors may be involved. In addition to the 'Sunken Idol', it appears a map was taken, perhaps with coded coordinates, that leads to a significant hoard of gold bullion."

Jack rubbed his temples. "Gold bullion? This sounds more like something out of a pirate movie."

"The Cold War never truly ended, Jack. Old rivalries, forgotten treasures, they all still hold immense power. We believe several nations, some with less than friendly intentions, are pursuing this lead."

Jack sighed, the weight of responsibility settling back on his shoulders. His beach vacation, a fleeting mirage, had vanished. "Alright, what do you need from me?"

"We need you on the ground. Discreetly, of course. Assess the situation, identify any potential leads. We believe the heist may be linked to a network operating in the Caribbean."

"Any other details?"

"The museum's security systems were bypassed with surprising ease. No witnesses, no forced entry. Clean in and clean out. We're sending you a package with the necessary credentials and cover identities. Expect a courier within the hour."

Jack hung up the phone, the cheerful sounds of Key West fading into the background. He stared at the wall, the image of the 'Sunken Idol,' a grotesque, gold-plated figure, flashing before his eyes. This was no ordinary heist. This was a game of international intrigue, a treasure hunt with deadly stakes.

He checked his watch. Time to get to work. The Mel Fisher Maritime Museum, here he came.

Jack arrived at the Mel Fisher Maritime Museum shortly after noon. The humid Key West air hung heavy, the vibrant colors of the island seeming a stark contrast to the somber mood that settled over him. He presented his credentials, a fabricated identity as a maritime historian researching the history of Spanish shipwrecks.

The museum's curator, a weathered man with eyes that held the wisdom of a thousand dives, greeted him with a mixture of suspicion and curiosity. Jack, with his practiced charm and a healthy dose of intimidation, quickly gained the man's trust.

"A devastating loss," the curator sighed, gesturing towards the empty display case where the Sunken Idol had once resided. "Such a magnificent piece." He trailed off, the weight of the loss echoing in his head.

Jack pressed him. "Any theories on who might have pulled this off?"

The curator shrugged. "Could be anyone. Local thieves, perhaps. Though the sophistication of the heist… it suggests something more. Maybe a foreign faction. The Cubans, perhaps. Or the Spanish. They've always had a keen interest in these waters."

Jack probed deeper. "Any known rivalries? Diving groups, treasure hunters?"

"Oh, there are plenty of those," the curator chuckled dryly. "The 'Sea Serpents,' a local group, they've been known to push the boundaries. And then there are the 'Deep Divers,' a more enigmatic group. They operate in the shadows, always searching for the next big find."

Jack thanked the curator, his mind racing. Cubans, Spaniards, rival treasure hunters, the list of suspects was growing. But one detail lingered: the escape. The curator had mentioned a fast powerboat heading west, towards Fort Jefferson and the Dry Tortugas.

Fort Jefferson. A massive, 19th-century fortress built on a cluster of small islands. Remote, isolated, and the perfect hideout for someone looking to disappear.

Jack needed to get closer. He headed to the local marina, his heart pounding. He needed a boat, and fast. A sleek speedboat would be ideal, but his options were limited. Finally, he settled on a skipjack, a traditional sailing vessel with a shallow draft, perfect for navigating the shallow waters around the Dry Tortugas.

"You sure about this, mister?" the grizzled old captain eyed him skeptically. "These waters can be tricky. And that skipjack, she ain't exactly known for her speed."

Jack grinned. "Perfect. Low profile. Less likely to attract attention."

The captain, intrigued, agreed to the charter. As they set sail, Jack realized this investigation was about to take a decidedly old-school turn. He was trading in his usual arsenal of high-tech gadgets for the unpredictable whims of the wind and the sea.

The salty air whipped through his hair, the familiar thrill of the chase returning. He might be out of his element, but Jack had never shied away from a challenge. This challenge rested on his ability to navigate both the treacherous waters of the Florida Keys and the murky depths of international intrigue.

The salty air whipped through Jack's hair as the skipjack, the "Salty Dog," sliced through the turquoise waters of the Florida Straits. Captain Silas, a weathered man with a mischievous glint in his eye, leaned against the mast, his gaze fixed on the horizon.

"You know," Silas began, his voice a low rumble, "this island, Key West, she's seen a lot of history. Spaniards, British, Americans… everyone wanted a piece of this rock. Strategic location, you see. Gateway to the Caribbean, a watchful eye on the Gulf of Mexico." He gestured towards the distant shoreline. "Back in the day, this was a haven for pirates, smugglers, you name it. Every empire, they've left their mark on this place."

Jack, intrigued, leaned forward. "And what about the Dry Tortugas? What's the story there?"

Silas chuckled. "Fort Jefferson, that's a story in itself. Built by the US government, meant to be an impenetrable fortress. But it mostly housed prisoners, some of 'em hardened criminals, some of 'em… well, let's just say they weren't exactly model citizens."

He paused, a thoughtful expression crossing his face. "You know, there's a whole underworld down here, beneath the surface. Treasure hunters, smugglers, you name it. There's the 'Sea Serpents,' like I mentioned, a bit rough around the edges, but mostly harmless. Then there's the 'Deep Divers.' Now, those guys, they're a different breed. Always shrouded in mystery, always pushing the limits. Some say they're funded by shadowy organizations, others say they're just a bunch of eccentric millionaires with a thirst for adventure."

Jack, absorbing the information, leaned back against the railing. "If you had to guess, Captain, who might be behind this theft?"

Silas stroked his chin. "My gut tells me this ain't no local job. Something deeper, something… international. Maybe the Cubans, trying to prove a point, maybe the Spaniards, getting a little payback for old times' sake. Or maybe… maybe someone's trying to embarrass the Americans, show them they can't even protect their own backyard."

He paused, a sly grin spreading across his face. "But let's be honest, at the end of the day, it's about the gold. Whoever finds that bullion, they'll be rich beyond their wildest dreams."

Jack nodded, his gaze fixed on the distant horizon. Fort Jefferson loomed closer, a brooding presence against the azure sky. He had a feeling this investigation was about to get a whole lot more complicated.

As the Salty Dog glided through the turquoise waters, Fort Jefferson emerged from the haze, a majestic, brooding presence. The massive stone walls, weathered by centuries of storms and salt spray, seemed to whisper secrets of the past. Jack, captivated, traced the shoreline with his gaze. The windward side, battered by the relentless waves, was a stark contrast to the leeward side, where pristine beaches beckoned.

He scanned the island, searching for signs of human activity. Tracks in the sand, discarded debris, anything that might offer a clue. The fortress itself, a silent sentinel, offered little in the way of clues. No visible signs of forced entry, no obvious signs of recent habitation.

As the Salty Dog tacked against the wind, an unfamiliar scent caught Jack's attention – a faint trace of woodsmoke from a pine tree. He sniffed the air, his senses heightened. A plume of smoke, barely visible against the azure sky, drifted lazily towards them.

"Captain," Jack said, his voice low, "did you see that?"

Silas, his eyes narrowed, followed Jack's gaze. "Smoke? That's odd. There's a small cove on the leeward side, sheltered from the wind, often used by, well, let's just say it's a popular spot for certain activities." He paused, a flicker of unease in his eyes. "Boy Scouts camping in the summer, that's the official story. But I wouldn't be surprised if it sees other visitors."

"We should investigate," Jack said, his voice firm.

Silas hesitated. "I don't like the feel of this, Jack. Something's not right."

Jack understood. There was a palpable tension in the air, an unseen presence lurking just beyond their sight. "I'll be cautious. I'll scout the area on foot."

"Be careful, Jack," Silas warned. "The water's deep here, and the currents can be unpredictable."

Jack nodded, his mind racing. He slipped on his wetsuit, the neoprene a comforting barrier against the cool water. Taking a deep breath, he launched himself overboard. The water was crystal clear, the sunlight filtering through, illuminating the vibrant coral reefs below. He swam towards the shore, his heart pounding, anticipation and apprehension battling for dominance. The adventure was truly underway.

Jack surfaced, gasping for air, and quickly swam towards the shoreline. He found a cluster of rocks, providing a decent cover. Peeking through the foliage, he spotted the campfire. Three men sat around it, their faces illuminated by the flickering flames.

Their accents were a fascinating tapestry: a thick Cuban lilt, a cultured Spanish cadence, and a gruff American drawl.

"This map… it's a devil," the Cuban grumbled, "confusing as hell."

"Patience, amigo," the Spaniard countered, his voice smooth as silk. "The treasure waits for no one."

The American, chewing on a cigar, scoffed. "These old maps, they're all riddles. Half the time, they're not even real."

"Real enough to get us here, isn't it?" the Spaniard retorted. "And don't forget, this island… it holds secrets. Tunnels, they say.

Built by those Yankee soldiers, hidden deep within the fortress."

The Cuban scoffed. "Tunnels? More likely rat holes."

"Perhaps," the Spaniard conceded, "but perhaps not. This island has seen empires rise and fall. Who knows what treasures lie buried beneath its surface?"

The conversation grew heated, each man vying for dominance, each driven by a different ambition. The Cuban, it seemed, was motivated by national pride, a desire to bring glory to his homeland. The Spaniard, by a thirst for wealth and a long-standing rivalry with the Americans. The American, simply by the allure of the unknown, the thrill of the hunt.

It became clear that this wasn't just a simple heist. This was a collision of interests, a dangerous game played by shadowy figures across the globe. They had colluded, perhaps unknowingly, representing factions, organizations, all driven by the same insatiable greed, the gold.

Jack watched as the three men rose to their feet, the embers of the fire dying down. They retrieved a small rowboat from the shoreline and began to row towards the opposite side of the island, disappearing as the sun shifted.

Jack waited until they were out of sight, then cautiously approached the campsite. The scene was a mess of discarded rations, empty water bottles, and crumpled maps. He found the Sunken Idol, covered in sand, seemingly in a temporary spot. It was surprisingly light, its gold surface tarnished. And there, nestled amongst the debris, he found something – a piece of parchment, frayed at the edges, covered in cryptic symbols and faded ink.

A crude map, drawn on goatskin, depicting the island of Dry Tortugas. But this wasn't any ordinary map. It showed hidden coves, unmarked trails, and most intriguing of all, a series of dotted lines leading towards the heart of Fort Jefferson.

The gold, it seemed, wasn't buried at sea. It was hidden somewhere within the fortress itself. And Jack Dolan, caught in the crosshairs of a global conspiracy, was about to delve deeper into the heart of darkness.

Jack, his heart pounding, carefully retrieved the Sunken Idol and the tattered map. He swam back to the Salty Dog, emerging from the water dripping wet and breathless.

Captain Silas, his eyes wide with concern, helped Jack aboard. "You alright down there?"

"Fine," Jack panted, handing Silas the Idol. "But we have a problem."

He unfolded the map, his finger tracing the dotted lines. "They're heading to the fortress. And I think I know where."

Jack explained his theory about the hidden tunnels. Silas, a seasoned sailor with a keen understanding of the island's secrets, nodded in agreement.

"There's a small cove on the other side of the island," Silas said, "a hidden inlet. The tides there… they create a natural opening, a kind of tidal pool. I've heard whispers of tunnels, old smuggling routes, leading from that cove deep into the fortress."

Jack's eyes gleamed with excitement. "That's it. We need to get there."

Silas expertly maneuvered the Salty Dog, the wind filling the sails as they tacked towards the hidden cove. Jack, armed with the map and a renewed sense of purpose, prepared for the final leg of his mission.

The cove, shrouded in the shadows of the fortress walls, was eerily beautiful. The tide was receding, revealing a small, crescent-shaped beach and a dark, gaping hole in the cliff face.

"Here we are," Silas said, his voice low. "Be careful, Jack."

Jack nodded, a determined glint in his eyes. "Three hours. I'll be back here in three hours. I have also alerted folks back on shore and they should be here, too."

He slipped back into the water, the cool embrace a welcome sensation. He took a deep breath, the map tucked securely into his wetsuit. The tunnel beckoned, a dark, mysterious passage leading into the heart of the fortress. Jack, armed with courage and a healthy dose of trepidation, plunged into the darkness.

Jack entered the tunnel, the cool water swirling around him. He held his breath as the tidal surge receded, leaving him momentarily suspended in darkness. Then, with a whoosh, the water rushed back in, urging him forward.

The tunnel was a labyrinth, a serpentine passage carved into the living rock. He navigated through narrow corridors, his hands tracing the rough-hewn walls. The air grew thick and stale, the silence broken only by the rhythmic drip of water.

It felt strangely familiar, this journey into the unknown. Like his own life, a series of twists and turns, dead ends and unexpected breakthroughs. He'd spent years chasing shadows, deciphering cryptic messages, only to find himself lost in a maze of his own making.

The map, his guide, seemed to be leading him astray. Dead ends loomed, the tunnel narrowing into impassable crevices. He backtracked, retracing his steps, each movement a calculated risk. The initial surge of adrenaline had subsided, replaced by a creeping sense of unease.

The light, his lifeline, grew dimmer, swallowed by the encroaching darkness. Panic threatened to consume him, but he pushed it down, focusing on his breath, on the rhythmic sloshing of the water. Logic, his compass in this subterranean maze, guided his every move.

Then, he heard it – voices. Murmurs, whispers, echoing through the tunnel. He slowed his pace, his senses on high alert. The voices grew louder, closer. Frustration, anger, and a touch of fear laced their tones.

"Damn it all!" the Cuban's voice, thick with exasperation.

"Perhaps the map is a forgery," the Spaniard conceded, his voice laced with a hint of defeat.

"Or maybe someone beat us to it," the American grumbled.

Jack, heart pounding, crept closer. He found a small alcove, concealed by a curtain of seaweed, and peered through. The three men, their faces etched with frustration, sat huddled around a flickering lantern.

"This whole thing… it was a waste of time," the Cuban declared.

"Perhaps," the Spaniard agreed, "but we won't give up. We'll find another way."

Jack, his patience wearing thin, pulled out his firearm. "I suggest you reconsider," he said, his voice echoing through the cavern.

The three men whirled around, their faces a mixture of shock and anger.

"Who… who are you?" the Spaniard stammered.

Jack stepped out of the shadows. "Someone who knows what you're looking for."

He leveled his weapon at them. "Now, tell me. What have you found?"

The men exchanged nervous glances. "Nothing," the American muttered. "Just a lot of wasted time."

Jack examined the map again, his gaze lingering on the faded ink. "Nothing?" he repeated. "I don't think so."

He pointed to a specific symbol, a stylized bird perched on a branch. "This isn't a map to treasure," he said. "It's a map to freedom."

The men exchanged puzzled glances.

"This wasn't about gold," Jack continued. "It was about escape. A secret passage, designed to help Confederate soldiers evade capture, or perhaps Union soldiers seeking refuge."

The men looked at him, more annoyed than angry. Their dreams of untold riches shattered, their mission a colossal failure.

"Alright, alright," the Cuban grumbled, "Let's get out of here."

Jack, his weapon still trained on them, gestured towards the tunnel entrance. "This way."

As they moved through the tunnel, the light at the end growing brighter with each step, Jack couldn't help but feel a strange sense of satisfaction. He had thwarted their ambitions, exposed their folly. But as he emerged from the depths of the fortress, blinking in the sudden sunlight, he couldn't shake the feeling that he'd been chasing a ghost, a phantom treasure that never truly existed.

As they emerged from the tunnel, blinking in the sudden sunlight, a small speedboat, sleek and menacing, awaited them. On board, the new Deputy Director of the CIA, a woman with eyes that held the weight of a thousand secrets, regarded them with a mixture of amusement and approval.

"Jack," she said, a loud voice, "I trust your vacation is proving to be… eventful?"

Jack, a wry smile playing on his lips, shook his head. "Not exactly the relaxation I had in mind, ma'am."

"Indeed," she replied. "But I must admit, you haven't disappointed."

The three men, looking bedraggled and defeated, were ushered onto the boat. As they were led away, Jack exchanged a brief nod with the Deputy Director. "Consider this vacation extended, Jack," she said with a knowing smile. "On the Agency's dime, of course."

Jack watched as the speedboat, carrying his unexpected guests, sped away from the island. He turned to Captain Silas. "Ready to get back to Key West, Captain?"

Silas grinned. "As ready as I'll ever be."

The Salty Dog, with the wind filling its sails, glided back towards the vibrant hues of the island. Jack, leaning against the railing, felt a sense of calm wash over him. The adrenaline had subsided, replaced by a quiet satisfaction. He had faced a challenge, navigated the unknown, and emerged victorious.

Back at the Weatherstation Inn, Jack settled into his room, the sounds of the island drifting in through the open window. He picked up a paperback novel, a light mystery, and curled up on the bed. As the sun dipped below the horizon, painting the sky in hues of orange and purple, he allowed himself to relax.

The adventure was over, for now. The world, with all its intrigue and danger, could wait. For now, there was only the gentle rhythm of the waves and the rustling of palm trees putting Jack to sleep.

CARDINAL

The aroma of freshly ground Colombian beans hung heavy in the air, a comforting counterpoint to the usual sterile scent of the Agency. Jack Dolan, his face still tanned from the Key West sun, leaned back in his chair, the worn leather groaning in protest. Across the small, circular table, his colleagues, a motley crew of analysts, operatives, and tech wizards, listened intently as he recounted his latest adventure.

"And there I was," Jack drawled, "standing in the heart of Fort Jefferson, surrounded by these three goons, all of them tired from trying to make sense of the writings on the paper."

A low chuckle rumbled from Ben, the tech whiz, his fingers already tapping away at his laptop, undoubtedly pulling up Jack's mission file. "You know," Ben remarked, "if it weren't for your 'vacation' report, I'd have sworn that was a fever dream."

"Believe me, Ben," Jack said, "it was surreal. Those tunnels, the history, the sheer audacity of those guys, it was like something out of an old pirate movie."

"Speaking of pirates," Sarah, the analyst with the sharpest mind in the room, chimed in, "Did you find any actual treasure?"

Jack shook his head, a wry smile playing on his lips. "Just a lot of disappointment and a few close calls with some rather colorful characters."

"But you got the Idol back," Jade, the newest member of their team, pointed out, her eyes wide with admiration. "And you apprehended the suspects."

"Mission accomplished," Jack acknowledged, raising his coffee mug in a silent toast. "The real treasure, Jade," he continued, his gaze sweeping across the faces of his friends, "is this team. The camaraderie, the shared intelligence, the unwavering support. That's what makes us successful."

He leaned forward, his voice dropping to a conspiratorial whisper. "You know," he said, "back in the day, they used to call this place 'The Company.' But I think it's more than that. It's a forge. We come here, we're tempered in the fires of adversity, and we emerge stronger, sharper, ready to face whatever challenges come our way."

A comfortable silence followed, punctuated by the soft clinking of coffee cups and the rhythmic tapping of keyboards. Jack, lost in thought, gazed out the panoramic window. The Potomac River, a ribbon of silver, shimmered in the afternoon sun. Afar, the city of Washington D.C. stretched out before him, a tapestry of green parks and towering skyscrapers.

He remembered reading somewhere that George Washington himself, while overseeing the construction of a canal, had enjoyed this very view. The same view that now inspired him, fueled his determination to protect the nation, to safeguard the ideals upon which this country was founded.

A flash of red caught Jack's eye. A small, vibrant cardinal, unafraid, had perched on the window ledge, its beady black eyes peering curiously through the glass. It cocked its head, seemingly taking in the sights and sounds of the Agency before spreading its wings and disappearing into the lush greenery of the Langley woods.

As the sun began its descent, casting long shadows across the city, Jack felt a profound sense of satisfaction. He was surrounded by the best, a team of dedicated professionals, each a vital cog in the intricate machinery of national security. And together, they would face any challenge, no matter how daunting, no matter how complex.

The future, like the setting sun, promised new beginnings, new challenges, new victories. And Jack, refreshed and reinvigorated, was ready to embrace it all.

The air in the conference room crackled with a nervous energy that overcame the heat from the sun that came through the glass. Jack, back from his unexpected Key West adventure, addressed his team, the weight of an upcoming papal visit settling heavy on his shoulders.

"Alright, folks," he began, his voice firm yet measured, "we have a new mission, and it's one of the most critical we've ever undertaken." He gestured towards the whiteboard, where Sarah had meticulously outlined the Pope's itinerary. "Landing at Dulles, motorcade to Brookland, residence at the Catholic University, a meeting with the President at the White House, mass in tight quarters at St. Matthew's, the schedule is packed."

Jack circled the whiteboard with his finger. "Our objective is twofold: identify and mitigate any potential threats, and ensure the smooth and uninterrupted execution of every single event. This isn't just about security; it's about projecting an image of strength, of unwavering support for our allies."

Ben, his eyes glued to the intelligence feeds on his multiple screens, spoke up. "Potential threats, we're looking at everything from lone wolf extremists to foreign intelligence agencies. Russian, Chinese, Iranian, they all have the capability to cause disruption."

Jade, ever the pragmatist, added, "We need to consider cyber threats as well. Disrupting communications, spreading disinformation, even attempting to compromise Vatican systems."

Sarah, her brow furrowed in concentration, listed the potential troublemakers. "Known extremist groups, fringe religious factions, even disgruntled individuals with grievances. We can't afford to overlook anything."

Jack nodded, his gaze sweeping across the room. "Exactly. This requires meticulous planning, meticulous surveillance." He shared a list he had made:

1. **Enhance our intelligence gathering:** Deep dive into the activities of known spy rings and embassies operating in the DC area. Analyze their communications, monitor their movements, and identify any unusual activity.
2. **Bolster security measures:** Work closely with the Secret Service, the Metropolitan Police Department, FBI, and all relevant agencies to ensure the highest level of security at every location.
3. **Develop contingency plans:** Anticipate every possible scenario, from minor logistical hiccups to major security breaches.

A wave of exhaustion washed over him, but Jack pushed through it. This was a mission of immense importance, a test of their skills, their resilience, their very existence as the Agency.

He looked at his team, their faces a mixture of concern and determination. "Alright," he declared, a surge of adrenaline coursing through him, "let's get to work. But first," he added with a grin, "I think we deserve a reward. Ice cream on me."

A collective sigh of relief and a chorus of enthusiastic agreements followed. The weight of the impending operation, though immense, seemed a little lighter now. They had a plan, a team, and a mission. And they were ready.

The week before the Pope's arrival, Jack found himself standing outside the imposing gates of the Russian Embassy, a knot of tension forming in his stomach. This wasn't his first visit, but the stakes were higher now. The Pope's visit had put a spotlight on the city, and Jack knew he had to be on his guard. The event was an evening gathering of diplomats from around the city, a gesture of good will.

Jack flashed credentials to the guards, their eyes narrowing in suspicion. He'd expected as much. The Russian Embassy was a fortress, a bastion of secrecy, and Jack knew he was treading on thin ice.

Once inside, he navigated the labyrinth with a guide, his ears attuned to any whispers, any unusual sounds. The air was thick with an unspoken tension, a palpable sense of surveillance. He could almost feel the eyes of unseen observers boring into him.

He made his way to the reception desk, a young woman with a bored expression handing him a visitor's badge. He thanked her, his eyes scanning the room, searching for any interesting people or behaviors.

The embassy was bustling, diplomats scurrying about, visitors whispering in hushed tones. Jack mingled with the crowd, his eyes darting from one face to another, his ears straining to pick up any snippets of conversation.

The embassy ballroom was a sea of faces, a kaleidoscope of diplomats, dignitaries, and spies. Jack, blending seamlessly into the crowd, spotted his target – a man with the steely eyes of a veteran operative, a subtle tremor in his hands betraying the years of high-stakes operations.

He approached cautiously, a glass of champagne in hand. "Dimitri," he began, his voice low and conversational, "a pleasure."

Dimiri, startled, looked up. "Jack, to what do I owe this pleasure?"

Jack smiled, a practiced charm masking the underlying tension. "Just wanted to express my admiration for you and your country's work. Navigating the world today requires a steady hand, a strong resolve."

Dimitri, intrigued, took a sip of his champagne. "And what, if I may ask, does the esteemed Jack admire?"

"Strength in this world is important," Jack continued, "The Pope, he is also a man of strength and resolve." Jack replied, his voice dropping to a conspiratorial whisper. "Such a significant event, his visit. A testament to the power of faith, of diplomacy."

Dimitri's eyes narrowed. "And you, Jack, what role do you play in this 'testament'?"

Jack shrugged, feigning nonchalance. "Just ensuring the smooth running of the event, you understand. Making sure nothing untoward occurs."

Dimitri studied him for a long moment, his gaze unwavering. "Assurances, Jack. That's what I need. Assurances that this 'significant event' will proceed without incident."

Jack leaned closer, his voice a silken whisper. "Yes. This city, this nation, will extend the utmost respect to His Holiness. Disruptions, they serve no one's interests."

Dimitri, a flicker of doubt in his eyes, finally nodded. "I agree, Jack. A message of cooperation."

Jack raised his glass in a silent toast. "To cooperation," he echoed, his mind already racing. The game had begun, and the stakes, as always, were dangerously high.

Jack thanked Dimitri and took his leave. He had gathered little of value, but the engagement had been invaluable to send the message.

Back at the Agency, he briefed his team, his voice low and urgent. "The embassy was buzzing. I connected with a known contact and he gave assurances the Russians will not interfere with the visit from the Pope. They are not interested."

"Any unusual activity?" Ben asked, his fingers already tapping away at his keyboard.

Jack shook his head. "Nothing concrete yet. But I felt eyes on me the entire time.

Sarah, her brow furrowed in thought, suggested, "Perhaps we need to move on to bolstering security measures by strengthening with other internal agencies and groups. Maybe we should focus on networks and contacts."

Jack nodded, a spark of inspiration lighting up his eyes. "I agree. Let's move onto signal intelligence in coordination with the other groups now."

The team fell silent, each member lost in thought, contemplating the complexities of their mission. So far, things were quiet. They were a formidable team, united by a common purpose, driven by a shared determination to protect their nation.

As the sun began to set, casting long shadows across the city, Jack looked out the window, his gaze fixed on the city below. He knew they had a long road ahead, but he also knew they had the skills, the resources, and the unwavering support of cooperating teams to overcome any obstacle.

The tension in the Situation Room was palpable. Days away from the Pope's arrival, the team was a finely tuned machine, each member a cog in the intricate web of security. Jack, pacing before the whiteboard, felt the weight of responsibility pressing down on him. This wasn't just about protecting a religious leader; it was about safeguarding the very fabric of international relations.

"Contingency plans," he barked, his voice echoing in the otherwise silent room. "Every possible scenario must be accounted for."

Ben, his eyes glued to a series of intricate maps and schematics, began. "We have agents positioned at every critical juncture: around the motorcade routes, at the university, at St. Matthew's. Observers are in place, snipers are on rooftops, ready to respond to any threat."

"Travel routes," Jade interjected, pointing to a map of the city. "Primary routes, secondary routes, emergency detours. We've coordinated with local law enforcement, traffic control, everything."

Sarah, ever the analyst, added, "We've studied the city's daily rhythms. Traffic patterns, pedestrian flows, even the typical bird migrations in the area. We're looking for anomalies, anything out of the ordinary."

Jack nodded, satisfied. "Good. Now, let's review the threat assessments. Who's on point for the Russian Embassy?"

Ben pulled up a file on his screen. "We've been monitoring their communications closely. No unusual activity detected, but we're still analyzing intercepted messages."

"What about the Chinese?" Jack pressed.

"Increased activity around the embassy," Jade reported. "We're seeing an uptick in encrypted communications, possible code word usage. We're working on deciphering the patterns. But nothing extraordinary to report."

The hours flew by as the team meticulously reviewed every detail, every contingency. They discussed crowd control measures, medical protocols, even the possibility of natural disasters.

Finally, as the sun began to set, casting long shadows across the room, Jack addressed his team. "We've done everything we can. Now, we wait. Stay vigilant, stay alert. And remember, we are a team. We stand together."

A sense of quiet determination settled over the room. They were ready. The stage was set. The world watched. And Jack, along with his team, stood guard, ready to face whatever challenges lay ahead.

The Pope's visit was imminent, and with it, the culmination of weeks of meticulous planning and tireless effort. The weight of the world, for the next few days, rested squarely on their shoulders.

But Jack, despite the looming pressure, felt a strange sense of calm. He had faith in his team, in their abilities, in their unwavering commitment to duty. They were ready. They were prepared. And they would not fail.

The Situation Room at Langley was a hive of activity. Monitors flickered with live feeds from across the city, mapping the Pope's every move. Signal intelligence analysts, their faces illuminated by the glow of computer screens, intercepted and analyzed every communication, sifting for the slightest anomaly. Agents in the field, their eyes and ears on the ground, reported in real-time, their voices crackling over secure channels.

Jack, his gaze fixed on the main monitor, watched as the Pope's plane touched down at Dulles International Airport. A collective sigh of relief rippled through the room. The first hurdle had been cleared.

The motorcade, a gleaming serpent of black vehicles, snaked its way through the city, a sea of cheering faces lining the route. The Pope, his face radiant with a gentle smile, waved to the crowd, his presence a beacon of hope in a world often shrouded in darkness.

The Situation Room buzzed with activity. "No anomalies detected," reported one analyst. "All signals within normal parameters."

"Crowd control is holding," another confirmed. "No signs of any disturbances."

As the day progressed, the Pope's itinerary unfolded flawlessly. The visit to Brookland passed without incident. The city, usually a cauldron of urban energy, seemed to hold its breath, a reverent hush falling over the usually bustling streets.

The night passed without incident. Jack and his team, fueled by adrenaline and caffeine, remained vigilant, their eyes glued to the monitors. Every shadow, every whisper, was scrutinized, analyzed, and dismissed. By dawn, exhaustion began to creep in, but no one dared to relax.

The morning brought a renewed sense of purpose. The last meeting between the Pope and the President, a private affair held within the White House, was a poignant moment. The two leaders, men of immense power and responsibility, spoke of global good, of reducing poverty, of feeding the hungry, of finding common ground in a world often divided by conflict.

"The only way to true peace," the Pope had declared, his voice resonating with a profound sense of conviction, "is to recognize the inherent goodness in all of humanity, to find common ground with our neighbors, regardless of their faith, their race, their nationality."

The afternoon brought the final event of the visit: the mass at St. Matthew's. A sea of worshippers, their faces uplifted, filled the square. A row of nuns, their white habits a stark contrast against the vibrant hues of the crowd, sat in the front row, their prayers a silent testament to their unwavering faith.

Jack and his team, their senses on high alert, monitored the proceedings with unwavering focus. No threats materialized. The mass proceeded peacefully, a symphony of voices raised in praise.

But as the Pope emerged from the church, a commotion erupted. A lone figure, standing amidst the crowd, yelled out, "Guy Fawkes!"

The Situation Room erupted in a flurry of activity. "What is happening?" Jack barked, his voice cutting through the din.

Radio traffic crackled to life, agents on the ground reporting the incident. Authorities swarmed the man, subduing him without incident.

Relief washed over the Situation Room. The man, it turned out, was homeless, and frequented the area, known for his eccentric behavior. He had yelled out the name in jest, a misguided attempt at humor, not really knowing the consequence.

News of the incident reached the Pope. He paused, his face etched with concern, and inquired about the man's well-being. Upon learning that the man was unharmed, he made a surprising decision. He instructed his security detail to bring him to him.

The crowd watched in stunned silence as the Pope, a symbol of peace and forgiveness, approached the trembling man. He placed a hand on his shoulder, his eyes filled with compassion. "It is alright," he said, his voice gentle. "Fear not."

The homeless man, overwhelmed by the unexpected encounter, fell to his knees, tears streaming down his face. "Forgive me, Father." he said.

The Pope, his face radiating with an otherworldly glow, blessed the man, his touch a balm to the troubled soul. He then returned to his vehicle, a wave of silence and awe washing over the crowd.

The Pope's visit, despite the brief scare, had been a resounding success. He had touched the hearts of millions, a beacon of hope in a world desperately in need of compassion and understanding.

As the papal motorcade sped down Rhode Island Avenue, heading back to Dulles and the confines of Rome, Jack and his team breathed a collective sigh of relief. The mission was complete. Peace had prevailed.

The Situation Room, usually a hive of activity, was eerily quiet. The adrenaline that had fueled them through the Pope's visit had subsided, leaving behind a palpable sense of exhaustion and a strange, almost unsettling calm.

Jack, leaning back in his chair, gazed out the window, watching the sun dip below the horizon, painting the sky in hues of orange and purple, his favorite time of day. A sense of peace, a rare and precious commodity in their line of work, had settled over the city. A red cardinal had returned, finding a place to perch on the sill.

"It's different," Sarah observed, her voice barely a whisper. "The city feels lighter."

Ben nodded in agreement. "Even the traffic seems to be moving slower, more deliberately."

Jade, ever the pragmatist, pointed out, "The Pope's message resonated with people. It reminded them of the importance of compassion, of understanding."

Jack, lost in thought, remembered the homeless man, his face etched with remorse, his soul touched by the Pope's unexpected act of kindness. It was a powerful reminder that even in the darkest corners of the world, there was always hope for redemption, for healing.

They spent the next few hours reviewing the mission, analyzing every detail, every intercepted communication, every movement tracked. The report would be lengthy, detailed, a testament to their meticulous planning and unwavering execution. But more importantly, it would serve as a reminder, a testament to the power of human connection, of the enduring spirit of hope that could transcend even the most challenging circumstances.

As the night deepened, Jack felt a wave of nostalgia wash over him. He remembered his time at the training center, the camaraderie, the shared experiences, the late-night discussions fueled by strong whiskey and even stronger convictions.

He reached into a hidden compartment in his desk, pulling out a small bottle of Virginia whiskey, a gift from an old friend. He poured out a few shots, passing them around the room.

"To a mission well executed," he said, raising his glass.

His team, their faces lit by the warm glow of the whiskey, echoed his sentiment.

"To peace," Sarah added.

"To hope," Ben chimed in.

"To humanity," Jade concluded.

Jack raised his glass. "To humanity," he echoed, his voice filled with a newfound sense of purpose.

And then, they drank. They laughed. They shared stories, reliving the tense moments, the unexpected turns, the shared triumphs. In that moment, surrounded by his team, Jack felt a profound sense of gratitude. He had found his calling, his purpose, in the service of his country, in the defense of freedom, in the unwavering pursuit of a better world.

As the night wore on, they sang "Auld Lang Syne," their voices echoing through the empty Situation Room, a testament to their enduring friendship, their shared victories, and their unwavering commitment to a future filled with hope and peace.

And as the final notes faded, a sense of contentment settled over them. They had faced a daunting challenge, they had overcome adversity, and they had emerged stronger, more united, more determined than ever before. The world, with all its complexities and dangers, awaited. And Jack Dolan, along with his team, was ready to face it.

DOMESTIC

The morning sun streamed through the window of Jack Dolan's bedroom, illuminating prisms on the wall from the glass of water on the nightstand. He stretched, the familiar aches and pains a testament to years spent chasing shadows, navigating the murky depths of international intrigue. The CIA, his second home for the past two decades, had become an extension of himself, a constant hum of activity, a tapestry woven with threads of intelligence, deception, and the ever-present threat of the unknown.

Jack had seen it all – the clandestine meetings in dimly lit cafes, the high-stakes chases through bustling city streets, the tense standoffs in foreign capitals. He'd faced down ruthless dictators, outmaneuvered cunning adversaries, and even, on occasion, saved the world from the brink of disaster. He was a legend in his own right, his name whispered with respect in the corridors of Langley, a ghost who moved through the shadows, a silent guardian of the nation's security.

His role was simple, yet crucial: to know. To know who the enemy was, to understand their tactics, to anticipate their moves. He was the eyes and ears of the Agency, a human spiderweb, collecting and analyzing intelligence from a myriad of sources – intercepted communications, covert surveillance, human intelligence gathered from a network of informants. He was the bridge between the raw data and actionable intelligence, the link between the shadows and the light.

But lately, the shadows seemed to be creeping closer, the light dimming. A growing wave of anti-government sentiment, fueled by misinformation and conspiracy theories, was sweeping across the nation. The CIA, once a symbol of American strength and resolve, was now painted as a shadowy organization, a puppet master pulling the strings of global events.

Jack scoffed, pouring himself a cup of strong black coffee. For years, he had dedicated his life to protecting his country, to safeguarding its interests against foreign threats. Now, it seemed, he had to defend himself, to defend the very institution he had sworn to uphold.

A news report crackled from the television, the voice of an elected official filling the room.

"The CIA," the politician declared, his voice laced with suspicion, "has infiltrated every aspect of our lives. They control the media, they manipulate elections, they even dictate our foreign policy. They are a danger to our democracy, a threat to our freedoms."

Jack shook his head, a bitter taste lingering in his mouth. For years, he had operated in the shadows, his actions shrouded in secrecy, his identity a closely guarded secret. Now, his work, his very existence, was under attack. The enemy, it seemed, was no longer lurking overseas. It was within, a insidious force that threatened to tear the fabric of the nation apart.

The challenge, Jack realized, was greater than any he had ever faced before. He had to not only protect his country from external threats but also defend it from the insidious whispers of doubt, from the erosion of trust that threatened to undermine the very foundations of their democracy and rule of law.

The politician's voice, amplified by the television, filled the room at Jack's house. "The CIA," he thundered, his voice dripping with contempt, "is a rogue organization, operating in the shadows, beyond the reach of the law. They meddle in foreign elections, overthrow democratically elected governments, and engage in covert operations that violate human rights."

Jack listened, his face a mask of grim determination. The politician, a skilled orator, weaved a tapestry of half-truths and outright lies, painting the CIA as a malevolent force, a threat to American democracy. He cited dubious examples – the Bay of Pigs invasion, the Iran-Contra affair, exaggerated claims of CIA involvement in foreign coups – twisting history to fit his narrative.

Jack closed his eyes, the bitter taste of betrayal lingering in his mouth. This wasn't just political rhetoric; it was a calculated attack, a deliberate attempt to undermine the very foundation of the Agency. These words, amplified by the media, were seeping into the public consciousness, eroding trust, sowing seeds of doubt.

He thought back to the origins of the CIA, born from the ashes of World War II, a successor to the Office of Strategic Services, the OSS. The OSS, a collection of brilliant minds and daring operatives, had played a pivotal role in defeating the Axis powers. They had gathered intelligence, conducted sabotage missions, and even organized resistance movements behind enemy lines.

The CIA, built upon the legacy of the OSS, had evolved, adapting to the ever-changing geopolitical landscape. They had thwarted countless terrorist plots, prevented nuclear proliferation, and protected American citizens from foreign threats. They were a shield, a guardian, a silent sentinel watching over the nation.

But now, that shield was being tarnished, the image of the Agency distorted by fearmongering and misinformation. The very people they swore to protect were being turned against them.

Jack took a long sip of his coffee, the bitterness mirroring the taste of betrayal that lingered in his mouth. He had dedicated his life to this agency, to upholding its mission, to protecting the values that underpinned American democracy. Now, those values were under attack, not from foreign adversaries, but from within.

He knew he couldn't allow this to stand. He had to fight back, not just for the Agency, but for the truth, for the very soul of the nation. He wondered, could the truth set things free?

The politician, emboldened by the applause of his supporters, continued his tirade. "And let's not forget," he boomed, his voice resonating through the auditorium, "the CIA's little playground in the Virginia woods. Prince William Forest Park, a seemingly innocuous expanse of green, is in reality a hub of clandestine activity."

Jack, sipping his coffee, felt a shiver run down his spine. Prince William Forest Park. He knew it well, a vast expanse of wilderness south close to the Potomac River, a place of tranquility and solitude. But to this politician, it was something else entirely.

"Coincidence?" the politician scoffed. "I think not. Situated mere miles from Quantico, the breeding ground for military intelligence, and a stone's throw from the FBI Academy, a fortress of domestic surveillance. Is this a mere coincidence, or is it a deliberate orchestration, a silent testament to the CIA's insidious reach?"

The crowd roared in approval. Jack, however, felt a growing sense of unease. The politician was spinning a dangerous narrative, weaving a web of conspiracy theories that could have devastating consequences.

He thought of the countless hours he had spent in the field, gathering intelligence, protecting his country from real threats. He thought of his colleagues, dedicated professionals who risked their lives to keep Americans safe. And now, their work, their sacrifices, were being painted as sinister, their efforts portrayed as a threat to the very people they swore to protect.

The politician continued, his voice gaining momentum. "They watch us, they listen to us, they even manipulate us. They are a shadow government, pulling the strings, controlling our destinies."

Jack closed his eyes, the weight of the accusations pressing down on him. He had sworn an oath to protect his country, to uphold its values. But now, he was being made to feel like a traitor, a conspirator in a vast, malevolent scheme. The man he had sworn to serve, the very people he had sworn to protect, were turning against him.

He took another sip of coffee, the bitter taste a stark reminder of the reality he now faced. The fight, he realized, was no longer just about defending the Agency from foreign threats. It was about defending the truth, about restoring faith in the very institutions that were meant to protect them.

The politician's voice continued, echoing through the auditorium, a chilling reminder of the growing distrust, the deepening chasm between the people and the government they were sworn to serve. Jack, his resolve hardening, knew he had a fight on his hands. A fight not just for the CIA, but for the soul of the nation.

Jack sat with his coffee, the politician's venomous words echoing in his mind. Fear, suspicion, and distrust were now the dominant narratives surrounding the CIA. He knew that simply denying the accusations wouldn't be enough. The public needed to see the truth, to understand the complexities of the Agency's mission, to appreciate the sacrifices made to keep them safe.

Two paths emerged in his mind. First, the Agency needed to acknowledge its past mistakes. Not to wallow in self-pity, but to be transparent, to own the errors, and to demonstrate a commitment to accountability. The public needed to see that the CIA was not a monolithic entity, that it was composed of fallible human beings who sometimes made mistakes.

Secondly, the Agency needed to counter the misinformation with a powerful narrative, a compelling story that showcased its true mission. They needed to highlight the countless successes, the lives saved, the threats averted. They needed to show the American people that the CIA was not their enemy, but their shield, their guardian.

Jack knew he couldn't do this alone. He needed an ally, someone with the credibility and influence to reach the American people. Someone who understood the importance of a strong national defense, someone who could cut through the noise and deliver the truth.

He thought back to his missions, the countless individuals he had encountered, the fleeting connections forged in the heat of the moment. One name surfaced from the depths of his memory: Senator William Grayson, a towering figure in Virginia politics, a staunch advocate for national security.

Senator Grayson, a man of integrity and conviction, had always been a strong supporter of the intelligence community. He understood the complexities of the world, the ever-present threat of adversaries, and the crucial role the CIA played in safeguarding the nation.

Jack picked up the phone, his fingers hovering over the familiar number. He took a deep breath, steeling himself for the conversation.

"Senator?" a voice answered, a hint of weariness in its tone.

"Senator Grayson," Jack began, his voice firm, "this is Jack Dolan."

A pause. "Jack… Dolan?"

"Yes, Senator. I… I need your help."

Senator Grayson, the senior senator from Virginia, the lines etched on his face a testament to years of service, sat back in his leather-bound chair, the memory of Jack Dolan slowly surfacing. "Jack Dolan… the Pacific affair," he murmured, recalling the tense standoff with the Chinese, their insidious attempts to manipulate international organizations and gain control of vital sea lanes. "You were instrumental, weren't you?"

"I did what I could, Senator," Jack replied, his voice grave. "But that was then. Now, the threat is different. It's… internal."

Grayson's brow furrowed. "Internal? You mean… domestic?"

"Yes, Senator. Misinformation. Disinformation. It's being used to tear the Agency apart, to erode public trust."

Grayson leaned forward, his eyes narrowing. "I've seen it. The rhetoric, the accusations, it is reckless, dangerous. People are scared, Jack. Uncertain about the future. They're looking for something to believe in, someone to blame. And unfortunately, the CIA, with its history of secrecy, has become an easy target."

Jack nodded in agreement. "Exactly. They're exploiting our past, twisting the truth to fit their own narratives."

"What do you propose we do, Jack?" Grayson asked, his voice firm. "This isn't something we can ignore."

"We need to fight fire with fire, Senator," Jack said. "We need to tell the truth."

Grayson considered this. "The truth? But how? The Agency is bound by secrecy, by the need for discretion."

"I understand the limitations, Senator," Jack acknowledged. "But we can be strategic. First, we need to acknowledge our past mistakes. Not to apologize, but to be transparent, to demonstrate that we are not above reproach."

Grayson nodded slowly. "That's a start. But we need more. We need a counter-narrative, something to counter the lies and the fearmongering."

"Exactly," Jack said. "And that's where you come in, Senator. You have the credibility, the platform. You can speak to the American people, explain the true mission of the CIA, the sacrifices made to keep them safe."

Grayson pondered this, a thoughtful expression on his face. "You're suggesting I become the Agency's… spokesperson?"

"Not exactly," Jack clarified. "You would be an advocate, a voice of reason, someone who understands the complexities of national security, someone the public can trust."

Jack then turned to the specific example of Prince William Forest Park. "They're claiming the park is some sort of secret CIA base, a breeding ground for conspiracy for internal domestic surveillance. Absurd, isn't it?"

Grayson chuckled. "Indeed. It's a beautiful park. I've hiked those trails myself. Peaceful, serene."

"Exactly," Jack said. "We could use it as a case study. The park, once a training ground for the OSS during World War II, now a haven for nature. The proximity to Quantico is merely a coincidence, a geographical anomaly."

Grayson considered this, a glimmer of intrigue in his eyes. "Perhaps a public visit, visiting Prince William Forest Park, enjoying a leisurely hike, demonstrating to the American people that there's nothing sinister there, just nature. Now that's an idea. But I need time, Jack. Time to think, to strategize with others."

"Of course, Senator. I understand. When can we speak again?"

"Tomorrow," Grayson said. "Tomorrow morning. I need to do some research."

Jack thanked the Senator, a sense of relief washing over him. He had found an ally, a powerful voice that could help him restore the Agency's reputation, to counter the tide of misinformation that threatened to engulf them. The fight had just begun, but Jack knew, with Senator Grayson by his side, they had a fighting chance.

He hung up the phone, a determined glint in his eye. The truth, he believed, was a powerful weapon. And he was determined to use it to defend the Agency, to defend the nation, and to restore faith in the very institutions that were meant to protect them.

The phone rang, startling Jack from a restless sleep. He fumbled for the receiver, his heart pounding. It was Senator Grayson.

"Jack," the Senator's voice was grave, "I need to be honest with you. Things have escalated."

Jack sat up, a knot of apprehension tightening in his stomach. "What do you mean, Senator?"

"The political climate," Grayson explained, "it's volatile. This anti-government sentiment, it's spreading like wildfire. I need the support of my colleagues, even those who disagree with my views on certain issues."

Jack understood. The political landscape was a delicate ecosystem, a constant struggle for power and influence. "I understand, Senator. The last thing we need is to further divide the country."

"Exactly," Grayson sighed. "This politician, with his inflammatory rhetoric, he's gained a significant following. A dangerous following. I need their votes on several crucial bills, you know the drill. If I alienate them now, if I publicly challenge their narrative, it could jeopardize everything."

Jack felt a wave of disappointment wash over him. The Senator could not have the public confrontation.

"I understand, Senator," Jack said, his voice subdued. "We need to address this, and we need to do it soon."

"I won't forget, Jack," Grayson assured him. "But for now, I need to lie low. A month, perhaps? Let things cool down. Let the dust settle."

Jack knew he had no choice but to agree. "A month. But I expect to hear from you soon, Senator."

"You will," Grayson promised. "Until then, stay safe."

Jack hung up the phone, the weight of the situation heavy on his shoulders. The fight, he realized, was far from over. The enemy was entrenched, the battle lines drawn. But he would wait. He would bide his time, gather his strength, and prepare for the inevitable confrontation.

The truth, he knew, would eventually prevail. But for now, he would play the long game, patiently waiting for the right moment to strike.

As Jack turned on the TV, an anchorman began to speak.

"A man armed with guns and ammunition was apprehended yesterday in Prince William Forest Park near the Breckenridge Reservoir. Authorities say Bradley Knight, a 42-year-old resident of Stafford County, Virginia, entered the park with the intent to expose what he believed to be a secret CIA base operating within its boundaries.

The incident began when a group of Boy Scouts camping in the park's backcountry encountered Mr. Knight. According to the scouts, Mr. Knight engaged them in a lengthy conversation about his suspicions, claiming the CIA was using the park for illegal surveillance operations against American citizens.

Alarmed by Mr. Knight's behavior and the presence of firearms, the scouts immediately contacted local authorities. A joint operation involving the local police and the FBI was launched.

Law enforcement officials established a perimeter and engaged in a standoff with Mr. Knight, who remained holed up in a remote area of the park. During the standoff, Mr. Knight reportedly made several statements about the CIA's alleged domestic surveillance activities, echoing conspiracy theories that have gained traction in recent months.

After two days of negotiations, with law enforcement officials employing psychological tactics to wear down Mr. Knight, authorities moved in. Mr. Knight, apparently exhausted and dehydrated, was taken into custody without incident.

Mr. Knight has been charged with multiple federal offenses, including illegal possession of firearms on federal land and making threats. The investigation is ongoing.

This incident comes amid a wave of anti-government sentiment and growing distrust of federal agencies."

Jack just shook his head.

The phone rang, startling. He fumbled for the receiver, his heart pounding. It was Senator Grayson, again.

"Jack," the Senator's voice was firm, "I'm at Prince William Forest Park right now."

Jack sat up, a jolt of adrenaline coursing through him. "At the park? Senator, what are you doing?"

"I'm giving a speech," Grayson replied. "A little impromptu press conference."

Jack's eyebrows shot up. "A speech?"

"Yes," Grayson continued, his voice calm and measured. "I believe it's time to set the record straight."

Jack listened intently as the Senator outlined his plan. He would begin by acknowledging the Agency's past mistakes, the missteps and overreaches that had eroded public trust. He would be honest, forthright, acknowledging the complexities of the Agency's mission, the inherent need for secrecy in certain operations.

Then, he would turn his attention to Prince William Forest Park. "I'm going to tell them the truth, Jack," Grayson said. "That it's just a park. Beautiful, peaceful. A place for families to enjoy, for hikers to explore. I'll even take a short hike with the press, show them firsthand that there's nothing sinister here, just nature."

Jack smiled. It was a bold move, a calculated risk. But it was exactly what they needed – a direct, honest confrontation with the misinformation that had been poisoning the public discourse.

"And finally," Grayson continued, "I'm going to address the broader issue. The erosion of trust, the spread of misinformation. I'm going to urge the American people to be critical thinkers, to question narratives, to seek out the truth from multiple sources. To remember that we are all Americans, and that we must strive to understand each other, to respect each other, to love each other."

Jack felt a surge of gratitude wash over him. The Senator was not just defending the Agency, he was defending democracy itself, reminding the American people of their shared values, their common humanity.

Jack sat back in his chair, a sense of satisfaction washing over him. The Senator's speech, bold and direct, was a powerful counter-narrative, a beacon of truth in a sea of misinformation.

He turned on the television, eager to hear the Senator's address. As the Senator spoke, his words resonating with conviction, Jack felt a renewed sense of hope. The fight was far from over, but he knew that with men like Senator Grayson, men of integrity and courage, they would prevail.

He sipped his coffee, a quiet smile playing on his lips. The truth, he realized, was a powerful weapon. And today, they had taken the first step towards reclaiming it.

CROWDS

The Potomac, a silver ribbon snaking through the heart of the nation's capital, mirrored the city's own serpentine nature. Washington D.C., a tapestry woven with history, politics, and power, pulsed with an undercurrent of secrets. Here, where the whispers of presidents echoed through marble halls and the ghosts of spies lingered in shadowed alleys, Jack Dolan, an experienced analyst for the Agency, was on the hunt.

Spring had descended upon the city, transforming it into a kaleidoscope of colors. Cherry blossoms, a delicate blush against the cerulean sky, blanketed the Tidal Basin, drawing tourists and locals alike. But beneath the surface of this idyllic scene, a different kind of bloom was taking place.

The arrival of spring in Washington D.C. coincided with the annual meetings of the World Bank and the International Monetary Fund, a magnet for diplomats, financiers, and, inevitably, spies. Foreign intelligence agencies, like predators circling prey, descended upon the city, their operatives mingling with the crowds, their eyes and ears ever alert for valuable intelligence.

Jack, hunched over his desk in the Agency's labyrinthine headquarters, watched the city unfold on his computer screen. Satellite imagery, real-time traffic feeds, social media chatter - all woven into a tapestry of information. He was searching for the subtle patterns, the fleeting anomalies that might betray the presence of foreign intelligence operatives. He was not doing domestic surveillance, but rather gathering intelligence on foreign agents operating in the US.

He knew the city well, its hidden corners, its back alleys, its parks teeming with secrets. He knew the history, the long shadow of espionage that had always loomed over Washington. From the days of the Cold War, when Soviet agents burrowed into the heart of government, to the modern era of cyber warfare and cyberespionage, the city had always been a battleground for intelligence agencies.

The city itself seemed designed for intrigue. The network of streets, the dense foliage of Rock Creek Park, the multitude of embassies and international organizations – all provided ample cover for clandestine meetings and covert operations. The sheer volume of people, the constant influx of visitors from around the globe, made it easy for spies to blend in, to disappear into the crowd.

Jack focused on the embassies, those opulent fortresses of stone and glass, each a microcosm of the nation it represented. He monitored their comings and goings, analyzing visitor logs, studying the patterns of their movements. He searched for the outliers, the individuals who deviated from the norm, who met in secluded locations, who exchanged coded messages.

He knew he was looking for needles in a haystack, but he was patient, meticulous. He had a knack for spotting the unusual, for connecting seemingly disparate pieces of information. He was a hunter, a shadow in the shadows, patiently stalking his prey.

The World Bank meetings had just begun, and the city was buzzing with activity. Jack knew that the next few weeks would be crucial. He would be working around the clock, analyzing data, following leads, piecing together the puzzle. He was determined to uncover the hidden networks, to expose the threats, to protect his city, his country, from those who sought to do it harm.

As the sun began to set, casting long shadows across the city, Jack leaned back in his chair, his eyes fixed on the cityscape. The lights of Washington D.C. twinkled like a million fireflies, a mesmerizing display of urban brilliance. But beneath the surface, a different kind of light was flickering – the cold, calculating light of espionage. And Jack, the silent observer, was determined to bring it to light.

The weight of history pressed down on Jack as he stared out the window of his office, the Washington Monument piercing the twilight sky. He thought of the countless spies who had prowled these streets, their shadows stretching long across the decades. Washington D.C., the nerve center of American power, had always been a magnet for intrigue, a city where secrets whispered on the wind and danger lurked beneath the surface.

The echoes of the past reverberated through his mind. The Cold War, a period of intense ideological struggle, had cast a long shadow over the city. Soviet agents, operating under deep-cover identities, had infiltrated government agencies, universities, and even social circles. One of the most notorious cases involved the Rosenbergs, Julius and Ethel, American citizens convicted of passing atomic secrets to the Soviet Union. Though their guilt remains a subject of debate, their execution in

1953 sent shockwaves through the nation, a stark reminder of the dangers of espionage.

The KGB, the Soviet Union's intelligence agency, had long considered Washington D.C. a prime target. They employed a variety of methods, from classic espionage techniques like dead drops and coded messages to more sophisticated methods of infiltration, exploiting human vulnerabilities and cultivating relationships with unsuspecting individuals.

But the threat wasn't always external. The specter of betrayal haunted the halls of power. Aldrich Ames, a senior CIA officer, was convicted in 1994 of spying for the Soviet Union and later Russia. He had compromised numerous CIA operations, causing irreparable damage to American intelligence gathering. Robert Hanssen, an FBI agent, was another devastating case. For years, he passed classified information to the Soviets and later to the Russians, betraying his country and endangering countless lives.

On the new digital front, the release of classified documents by WikiLeaks in 2010 and subsequent years sparked intense debate about government transparency, whistleblowing, and the role of the media in a democratic society. The disclosures of Edward Snowden in 2013, revealing the extent of global surveillance programs conducted by the U.S. government, further highlighted the evolving landscape of espionage and the challenges of maintaining privacy in the digital age.

These betrayals and releases, these moles within the heart of the intelligence community, had shaken the foundations of American security. They served as stark reminders of the human element of espionage, the vulnerability of even the most trusted individuals.

Jack thought of the countless other cases, the shadowy figures who had operated in the shadows of Washington D.C.: the Soviet defectors who sought refuge, the Cuban spies who attempted to infiltrate government agencies, and the Chinese intelligence officers who meticulously cultivated relationships with American officials.

Related, Jack remembered reading about the "Cambridge Five," a group of British spies who passed secrets to the Soviet Union during World War II. One of them, Kim Philby, had even infiltrated the British Secret Intelligence Service (MI6), becoming one of its most trusted officers while secretly feeding information to the Soviets.

The city itself seemed to whisper of these hidden histories. The grand avenues, the imposing government buildings, the elegant mansions – all held within their walls a tapestry of secrets, a history of intrigue and betrayal. Jack imagined the countless clandestine meetings that had taken place in these very streets, the whispered conversations, the furtive exchanges of information.

He knew that the game of espionage had evolved, becoming more sophisticated, more insidious. Cyber warfare, disinformation campaigns, and the exploitation of social media had become the new battlegrounds. But the core principles remained the same: deception, manipulation, and the constant struggle for information and the truth of that information.

As he prepared to delve deeper into his investigation, Jack felt a sense of awe mixed with apprehension. He was in a world of shadows, a world where appearances could be deceiving and trust was a rare commodity. He knew that he had to be vigilant, to question everything, to trust his instincts.

Jack leaned back in his chair, the rhythmic hum of the Agency a constant undercurrent. He was meeting with Jade, one of the newest members of the team, a bright-eyed young analyst who had helped him during the Pope's visit, who was now assigned to assist him with his investigation.

"Jade," he began, gesturing towards the panoramic window overlooking the Potomac, "let's talk about the cherry blossoms."

Jade, startled, blinked. "The cherry blossoms, sir? I thought we were discussing Chinese intelligence operations."

Jack chuckled. "We are. But understanding this city, its rhythms, its nuances, is crucial. And what better way to understand Washington D.C. than through one of its most iconic symbols?"

He launched into a brief history lesson. "You see, these cherry trees, a gift from the people of Japan in 1912, symbolize a delicate yet enduring friendship. But their history is intertwined with the city's own turbulent past. During World War II, when tensions between the US and Japan escalated, the very existence of these trees was questioned. Some even called for their removal, viewing them as a symbol of the enemy."

He continued, "But they remained, a testament to the enduring spirit of diplomacy and the hope for peace. Today, they are a symbol of renewal, a celebration of spring, a time for reflection and appreciation of beauty."

He gestured towards the monuments that lined the Tidal Basin. "Look at them. The Washington Monument, a testament to the founding fathers, soaring towards the heavens. The Jefferson Memorial, a tribute to the author of the Declaration of Independence. The FDR Memorial, a poignant reminder of a leader who guided the nation through some of its darkest hours. And the MLK Memorial, a monument to the dream of equality."

He paused, letting the weight of history settle. "This city, Jade, is a microcosm of the American experience, a tapestry woven with threads of hope, despair, triumph, and struggle. It's a city that has witnessed the birth of the nation and the ongoing struggles within and abroad."

He turned back to her, his eyes twinkling. "Now, tell me, when do you think the cherry blossoms will bloom this year?"

Jade, caught off guard by this unexpected turn, stammered, "I don't know, sir. When do they usually bloom?"

Jack smiled. "That's the thing, Jade. Predicting the bloom is a bit of an art. It depends on the weather, the temperature, and the amount of sunlight. It's a delicate dance between nature and the whims of the universe."

He leaned forward, his voice dropping to a conspiratorial whisper. "Just like intelligence gathering, isn't it? You never know when the information will bloom, when the opportunity will present itself. You have to be patient, observant, and always ready to adapt."

Jade, intrigued, nodded. "So, we're learning about espionage by studying cherry blossoms?"

Jack chuckled. "In a way, yes. Understanding the city, its rhythms, its hidden patterns, is crucial to our work. And what better way to understand a city than by observing an iconic symbol of both beauty and resilience."

He paused, his gaze sweeping across the cityscape. "Now, let's get back to work. Let's start researching the individuals who will be attending the World Bank meetings. Identify any potential points of interest, any anomalies in their travel patterns, any connections to known intelligence agencies."

Jade, her curiosity piqued, nodded eagerly. "Yes, sir. I'll get right on it."

As Jade delved into her research, Jack watched her, a flicker of pride in his eyes. He knew he had found a worthy partner, a young analyst with a sharp mind and an insatiable curiosity. Together, they would navigate the treacherous waters of espionage, one step at a time, one blossom at a time.

Jade, fueled by Jack's approach, dove headfirst into her research. Days blurred into nights as she sifted through mountains of data, her eyes glued to the computer screens. She spent hours with the signals intelligence unit, poring over intercepted communications, deciphering coded messages, and piecing together the puzzle.

Initially, the sheer volume of data was overwhelming. Countless conversations, both mundane and significant, flowed across the screens, a cacophony of voices and whispers. But Jade, with a patience that belied her youth, began to discern patterns. She identified key players, mapped their communication networks, and slowly, painstakingly, started to build a picture of the intelligence landscape.

Then, she stumbled upon it. A series of intercepted communications from a high-ranking Chinese official attending the World Bank meetings. The official was notorious for his meticulous preparations and his unwavering adherence to routine. But what struck Jade as odd were his frequent digressions, his obsessive chatter about his upcoming shopping trips to Tysons Corner Mall during the meetings.

"The new Gucci collection is arriving next week," he boasted in one communication.

"I simply must acquire that limited-edition Cartier watch," he declared in another.

At first, Jade found these interjections annoying, irrelevant distractions from the serious business of intelligence gathering. But then, a seed of suspicion was planted. Why this obsession with consumerism? Was it a deliberate attempt to mask the true purpose of his communications? Or was it a subtle form of signaling, a coded message embedded within seemingly innocuous chatter?

Jade decided to investigate further. She cross-referenced his communications with other intercepted data, searching for any patterns, any connections that might shed light on the meaning behind his shopping sprees. And that's when she found it.

A cryptic message, buried within a seemingly innocuous conversation about a new line of Italian shoes, hinted at a rendezvous. "The usual place," the message read, followed by a vague reference to "the third day of the meetings."

Jade's heart quickened. "The usual place." What did it mean? Where was this "usual place"? After hours of research, a chilling realization dawned on her. The Tidal Basin.

The cherry blossoms were in full bloom, a breathtaking spectacle of color against the backdrop of the Washington Monument. But for Jade, the beauty of the blossoms was overshadowed by a different kind of bloom, the clandestine operations that were about to unfold beneath their delicate petals.

She immediately informed Jack of her findings. He listened intently, his eyes gleaming with excitement. "A dead drop," he murmured, "at the Tidal Basin. Classic."

"But sir," Jade added, "He is obsessed with Tysons Corner. He'll be there, I'm sure of it. We can use this to our advantage."

Jack grinned. "Excellent thinking, Jade. We'll play a two-pronged game. You'll monitor the official's movements, track his every step, ensure he makes his pilgrimage to Tysons Corner. While you're doing that, I'll be at the Tidal Basin, observing the scene, looking for any signs of unusual activity."

"But sir, how will we know who we're looking for? The spy could be anyone."

"That's the challenge," Jack replied, "We'll have to rely on our instincts, our ability to read the crowd, to identify the anomalies, the fleeting moments of tension, the furtive glances. We'll be looking for the ghost in the crowd, the invisible hand that moves the pieces."

The third day of the World Bank meetings arrived, a day of high-stakes diplomacy and clandestine operations. As the city buzzed with activity, Jack and Jade prepared for their respective roles. Jade, armed with real-time intelligence feeds and a keen eye for detail, tracked the official's movements. He, as predicted, made his pilgrimage to Tysons Corner, indulging in a shopping spree that would have made even the most ardent consumer envious.

Jade alerted Jack that the official was on his way to the Tidal Basin after a full day of shopping at Tysons Corner.

Jack positioned himself discreetly along the banks of the Tidal Basin, his senses on high alert. He blended seamlessly with the crowd, observing the scene with a practiced eye. He watched tourists snapping photos, children chasing pigeons, lovers strolling hand-in-hand. But beneath the surface of this idyllic scene, a different kind of game was being played.

He waited, his patience unwavering, his senses attuned to the slightest shift in the atmosphere, the faintest tremor in the crowd. He knew that the encounter would be brief, a fleeting moment of contact, a silent exchange of information. He had to be ready, alert, his eyes and ears attuned to the subtle cues, the whispers of the unseen.

The shadows lengthened, the sun dipping below the horizon, casting long reflections on the still waters of the Tidal Basin. The cherry blossoms, illuminated by the fading light, seemed to hold their breath. And as the twilight deepened, Jack knew that the game was about to begin.

As the sun dipped below the horizon, the Tidal Basin transformed. The cherry blossoms, illuminated by the soft glow of the city lights, took on a surreal, almost ethereal quality. The Washington Monument, a beacon of white marble, pierced the twilight sky, its apex reflecting the fading light. The Jefferson Memorial, bathed in a warm, golden glow, stood serene and dignified. The FDR Memorial, with its cascading waterfalls and poignant inscriptions, evoked a sense of both grandeur and melancholy. And the MLK Memorial, a masterpiece of modern sculpture, stood as a testament to the ongoing struggle for justice and equality.

The air was alive with the sounds of the city – the murmur of conversations, the laughter of children, the distant hum of traffic. Tourists strolled along the promenade, their cameras flashing, capturing the magic of the moment. Lovers lingered, their arms entwined, whispering secrets in the soft evening breeze.

Jack, blending seamlessly with the crowd, observed the scene with a practiced eye. He watched a young couple, their faces illuminated by the soft glow of their phones, taking selfies in front of the Jefferson Memorial. He noted the elderly gentleman sketching the cherry blossoms with a practiced hand, his face a mask of concentration. He observed a group of schoolchildren, their voices a cacophony of excitement as they raced towards the water's edge.

Then, he saw them. A convoy of three black Suburbans, their windows tinted, pulled up to the curb near the Jefferson Memorial. A group of dignitaries, their faces obscured by the shadows, emerged from the vehicles and strolled along the promenade, their conversations hushed and guarded. Jack watched them closely, searching for any signs of unusual behavior, any fleeting moments of tension, any indication that this was more than just a casual stroll.

After a brief tour, the dignitaries returned to their vehicles and drove away. Jack realized it must have been the target he sought. Jack, his curiosity piqued, decided to investigate further. He approached the Jefferson Memorial, looking for clues, his gaze sweeping across the grounds. And then he saw it – a small, intricately folded origami bird lying at the foot of Thomas Jefferson.

He knelt down, his heart pounding. Carefully, he unfolded the bird. Inside, a second piece of paper was concealed. He deciphered the message: "The bags will be shipped in a few weeks in the trunks of the cars."

Jack's mind raced. "The bags." What did it mean? Drugs? Weapons? Classified documents? The possibilities were endless. He carefully placed the origami bird back where he found it and stepped back, observing the crowd.

A man, dressed in a nondescript suit, was standing a few feet away, his eyes fixed on the Jefferson Memorial. He took a hesitant step forward, his gaze darting around nervously. Then, he approached the statue, knelt down, and retrieved the origami bird. He slipped it into his pocket and quickly melted back into the crowd, disappearing into the Cherry Blossom crowd without a trace.

Jack watched him go, a wave of confusion washing over him. What had just happened? Was he the courier? Or was he simply a decoy, a red herring designed to mislead him?

He felt a tap on his shoulder. Jade stood beside him, her eyes wide with excitement. "Did you see that?" she whispered.

"See what?" Jack replied, his voice low.

"The cars, the dignitaries, the bird… it was all so… orchestrated."

Jack recounted his observations, his voice filled with a mixture of excitement and apprehension. "I think we just witnessed a dead drop, Jade. But I don't understand. Let's go back to the cars and discuss."

Silence initially overcame Jack and Jade as they were mentally reviewing what they saw. Finally, Jade broke the silence, "Were you able to read the note in the bird, sir?"

Jack nodded, his mind still reeling from the encounter. "Yes. 'The bags will be shipped in a few weeks in the trunks of the cars.'"

Jade's eyes widened. "I know what it means."

Jack leaned forward, intrigued. "You do?"

"Think about it," Jade explained, her voice rising with excitement. "This official is obsessed with luxury brands, he may be involved in an import-export operation. It's too obvious to be a coincidence. He's not smuggling secrets, he's smuggling merchandise, but secretly."

"Counterfeit goods?" Jack exclaimed, his mind racing. "High-end handbags, designer clothing, maybe even electronics. They're using the diplomatic immunity of these dignitaries to smuggle in counterfeit goods, evading customs and probably raking in millions."

"Exactly!" Jade exclaimed. "They're using the legitimate export of cars as a cover. The 'bags' aren't secret documents, they're shipments of counterfeit luxury goods hidden within the car trunks. In this case, they are bags!" They laughed.

This was espionage, but also a sophisticated criminal enterprise operating under the guise of diplomatic immunity.

"We need to get back to Langley," Jack said, his voice urgent. "We need to alert folks."

They raced back to Langley, the city lights blurring into streaks of color as they sped through the night. Jack and Jade gave a briefing, outlining their findings: the dead drop, the coded message, the official's obsession with luxury goods, and the connection to the counterfeit goods market.

The reaction was immediate. A team of investigators was assembled, including specialists in customs and border protection, financial crimes, and intelligence analysis. Jade, to Jack's immense pride, was appointed as the lead analyst to follow the clues on the next part of the case, her sharp mind and insightful observations proving invaluable. It was her case to close.

The investigation that followed was complex and multifaceted. They tracked the movements of the dignitaries, monitored their communications, and analyzed financial transactions. They infiltrated counterfeit markets, gathering intelligence on the distribution networks and identifying key players in the operation.

After weeks of meticulous investigation, they finally cracked the case. They intercepted a shipment of counterfeit luxury goods hidden within diplomatic vehicles, arresting the key players and dismantling the smuggling ring. The official, with a carefully constructed facade shattered, was apprehended and charged with a multitude of crimes.

The case garnered international attention, a testament to the ingenuity and dedication of the investigative team. Jack, watching from the sidelines, felt a sense of satisfaction. He had uncovered a sophisticated criminal operation, protected the integrity of international trade, and exposed a threat to the global economy.

But more importantly, he had mentored a young analyst, guiding her through the complexities of the intelligence world, fostering her growth and empowering her to make a significant contribution. As he watched Jade, her face radiating with pride and accomplishment, Jack knew that he had not only solved a case but also helped to shape the future of a promising analyst. The future of the Agency, he realized, was in good hands.

LISTENING

The worn map of Washington D.C. lay spread across the table in the small van, a vibrant tapestry of embassies woven into the city's fabric. Jack Dolan, his gaze sweeping across the intricate layout, pointed a finger towards the northwest corner. "See this stretch here, Ben? Along Rock Creek Park? That's where the magic happens."

Ben, his eyes glued to the map, leaned forward. "Embassy Row? All those fancy buildings, practically touching each other."

Jack nodded. "Exactly. Years ago, we realized something brilliant. These embassies, they're not just showpieces. They're nerve centers, humming with activity. Both diplomatic and clandestine. And many of them, right here, back up to the park. Gives us a unique advantage."

"The park?" Ben raised an eyebrow.

"Think about it," Jack explained. "Miles of trails, winding through dense foliage. Perfect for covert surveillance. We can get incredibly close, almost within earshot with good technology, without raising suspicion. We've been intercepting communications from these embassies for decades, building a massive database."

"But why? Why all this effort?"

Jack leaned back, a thoughtful expression on his face. "We're building a network, Ben. Not just of signals, but of relationships. Who's talking to whom? What are their patterns? This information, it's invaluable. It helps us connect the dots, understand the bigger picture. When another case comes along, a threat emerges, we'll have a head start. We'll know who to look at, who to listen to."

Ben, intrigued, began to see the bigger picture. "So, we're not just eavesdropping. We're mapping the entire intelligence landscape of Washington D.C."

Jack grinned. "Exactly. And the best part? We get to do it while enjoying some of the most scenic trails in the city." He glanced at his watch. "Speaking of which, time to put on our 'running shoes' and get to work."

Ben chuckled. "Trail running, huh? Sounds like a fun way to gather intelligence."

Jack winked. "The best kind, wouldn't you say?"

And with that, the two analysts rose from the table and opened the side door to the van, their eyes gleaming with a mixture of anticipation. The Rock Creek Park, with its hidden secrets and strategic advantages, awaited them.

The sun beat down on Jack and Ben as they navigated the intricate trail system of Rock

Creek Park. Hidden deep within their pockets, small, unobtrusive radios diligently scrolled through frequencies, their antennae twitching like nervous insects. Any signal, however faint, would be instantly locked onto, a digital whisper in the cacophony of the city.

Jack, his earpiece seemingly playing an invisible soundtrack, kept a watchful eye on the trail ahead. He timed his strides with the rhythmic beeps of the radio, each step a silent query into the ether. "You think the Nats are going to make the playoffs this year, Ben?" he asked casually, his voice a low murmur against the rustling leaves.

Ben, his brow furrowed in concentration as he checked his own radio, replied, "Hard to say. They've got the pitching, but the offense, well, let's just say it could use a boost." He grinned. "Besides, I'm more of a Caps fan myself."

Their conversation continued in this vein, a lighthearted banter about local sports teams, a perfect cover for their covert operation. They paused occasionally, leaning against a moss-covered tree or perched on a fallen log, their eyes scanning the surrounding foliage. Was that a fence line? A glimpse of an embassy building through the trees? Each observation was carefully noted, each pause an opportunity to analyze the radio signals, to filter out the static and isolate the whispers of intelligence.

Two hours flew by in a blur of motion and observation. Sweat trickled down their temples, their lungs burning with the exertion, but their spirits remained high. This was more than just a surveillance operation; it was a thrilling game of cat and mouse, a dance with the unseen.

As the sun began its descent, casting long shadows across the park, they decided to call it a day. The van, their mobile command center, awaited them at the trailhead.

"Well, that was a productive run," Ben said, panting slightly as they emerged from the trees.

Jack nodded, his eyes already scanning the horizon. "Indeed. Let's see what treasures we've uncovered."

They climbed into the van, the air-conditioning a welcome relief from the summer heat.

"Tomorrow, Langley," Jack declared, removing his earpiece. "We'll pour over those signals and see what secrets they hold." He paused, a mischievous glint in his eye. "You like linguine vongole?"

Ben chuckled. "Who doesn't? I'm in."

The "Listening Post" room, a sterile white room at Langley, hummed with a low, mechanical drone. Sunlight, filtered through the heavily tinted windows, cast long, eerie shadows across the bank of gleaming workstations. Jack and Ben, their faces grim, sat before a cluster of monitors, each displaying a different waveform, a chaotic dance of digital signals.

This was their workshop, the heart of their operation. Years of meticulous planning and cutting-edge technology had culminated in this room, a sanctuary for the unseen, a battlefield of bits and bytes.

At the center of the room, a massive server rack hummed like a caged beast, its internal fans churning a whirlwind of cool air. Within its depths resided the core of their system: a custom-built supercomputer, capable of processing terabytes of data in mere seconds.

Jack, a master of the arcane, began his ritual. With a few keystrokes, he activated the system, a cascade of green lights illuminating the server rack. On the primary monitor, a complex interface materialized, a tapestry of interconnected nodes and pathways.

"Alright, Ben," Jack said, his voice a low growl, "Let's see what we've caught."

He selected the first target: the Botswana Embassy. A series of filters were applied, designed to isolate human speech from background noise, to weed out the static and the whispers of the city. The waveform, previously a chaotic mess, began to resolve, revealing distinct patterns, the rhythmic cadence of human conversation.

"Interesting," Jack murmured, zooming in on a particular segment. "Sounds like a heated discussion. Let's listen in."

With a click, the audio playback initiated. A fragmented conversation emerged: "...sanctions...embargo...diamond mines..." The voices were muffled, distorted, but the underlying message was clear: a tense negotiation, likely concerning trade and international pressure.

Ben, his eyes glued to the secondary monitor, cross-referenced the audio with intelligence reports on Botswana's recent political developments. "Could be related to the recent coup attempt," he suggested. "They're probably scrambling to secure international support."

Jack nodded. "Good catch. Let's move on. Libya next."

The process was meticulous, painstaking. They navigated through a labyrinth of signals, each embassy a new puzzle to solve. The Netherlands, a flurry of diplomatic chatter; Kuwait, hushed conversations about oil prices; Hungary, a tense exchange regarding regional security.

As they progressed, a disturbing pattern began to emerge. A recurring theme: fear. Fear of instability, of economic collapse, of rising tensions. The world, it seemed, was teetering on the brink.

Hours bled into the afternoon. The sun dipped below the horizon, casting the room in a twilight gloom. Jack and Ben, fueled by caffeine and a shared sense of purpose, continued their relentless pursuit.

Finally, they reached the last two embassies: Sweden and Iceland, nestled together on an interesting geography at the mouth of the Potomac, called "The Mole", near C&O Canal mile marker 0, where Jack and Ben had turned around during their run. The signals from these embassies were weaker, more elusive, buried beneath the static of the city, and under heavy protection.

Jack, his eyes narrowed in concentration, manipulated the filters, coaxing the faintest whispers to life. A chilling realization dawned on him. These conversations, unlike the others, were not diplomatic exchanges. They were private, intimate, laced with a raw, primal fear.

"Listen to this, Ben," Jack said, his voice barely a whisper.

The audio playback began. A woman's voice, trembling with terror, emerged from the static: "There will be no truce. It is only a matter of time before they take it over."

Ben's blood ran cold. This was no ordinary intelligence gathering. And the truth they were uncovering, the terrifying truth, was far more than they had bargained for.

The chilling fragments of the Swedish conversation haunted Jack. He couldn't shake the image of a terrified woman, her voice a ghost in the machine, whispering of impending doom. This wasn't just about foreign policy; it was about the very fabric of European security.

"We need to go back, Ben," Jack said, his voice grave. "But this time, we're going closer."

Ben, still reeling from the unsettling audio clip, nodded. "Closer? How close?"

"As close as we can get without raising suspicion," Jack replied. "We're going to the waterfront, set up shop near the Swedish Embassy, the House of Sweden, as we act like we are going to go out on the river in a crew boat. We'll take our time, observe, listen and maybe even take that boat out in the Potomac."

The plan was audacious, bordering on reckless. But the stakes had been raised. This was no longer about routine surveillance; it was about uncovering a potential threat to global stability.

The following afternoon, they staked out a position on the waterfront, at the boathouse overlooking the Potomac. The House of Sweden, a modern structure of glass and steel, stood majestically across the river, a sentinel guarding the nation's interests.

They observed the comings and goings, noting the license plates of the cars, the faces of the visitors, the subtle nuances of their behavior.

Their radios, now modified with more powerful antennae, hummed with the faintest whispers of the embassy's internal communications. They focused their efforts, filtering out the noise, honing in on specific frequencies.

Time passed. As the sun moved, casting long shadows across the river, they decided to escalate their efforts. They prepared to take the double scull out of the boathouse, a sleek, elegant vessel designed for quiet exploration.

With practiced strokes, they glided across the water, taking their time around the embassy. The rhythmic motion of the oars provided the perfect cover for their eavesdropping. They listened intently, their ears straining to catch the faintest whispers carried on the breeze.

And then, they heard it. A hushed conversation, fragments of a chilling message: "The power in Europe is changing... the NATO alliance is weakening... as large, powerful countries are strengthening to slowly imagine taking over land, just like Germany did before World War II."

The words hung in the air, heavy with dread. Chills ran down Jack's back. This wasn't paranoia; this was a genuine fear, articulated by those on the front lines of European diplomacy.

Large countries like Russia, it seemed, were flexing their muscles, testing the boundaries of international law and respect for sovereignty. The specter of a new era of conflict, a return to a darker age of imperialism, loomed large.

Jack and Ben exchanged a grim look. Their casual surveillance mission had stumbled upon something far more sinister than they could have ever imagined. The world, they realized, was teetering on the precipice, and they were the unwitting witnesses to a gathering storm.

The Deputy Director, a woman whose face was etched with the weight of a thousand classified briefings, listened intently as Jack and Ben laid out their findings. The sterile conference room, usually buzzing with the low hum of activity, fell silent.

"So, you're saying," the Deputy Director said, her voice grave, "that European powers are genuinely concerned about a resurgence of aggressive expansionism?"

"Yes," Ben replied, "They fear a return to the dark days of the last century, a time when borders were redrawn with force, when sovereignty was trampled upon."

Jack added, "The language they use is chilling. Fear, uncertainty... a sense of impending doom." He then recounted the chilling phrase: "Just like Germany did before World War II."

The Deputy Director leaned back in her chair, brow furrowed. "This is serious, very serious. This isn't just about espionage; it's about the potential for global instability." She paused, her gaze sweeping across the room. "We need to tread carefully. We can't afford to provoke a crisis. But we need to be prepared."

"Prepared for what?" Ben asked.

"For anything," the Deputy Director replied. "We need to strengthen our alliances, improve our intelligence gathering, and be ready to respond to any threat, however unlikely it may seem." She looked at Jack and Ben. "This information is invaluable. You've done excellent work."

Jack and Ben exchanged a look. The gravity of the situation weighed heavily on them. They had stumbled upon something far greater than they had initially anticipated.

"Thank you," Jack replied. "We'll continue to monitor the situation closely."

As they left the conference room, a sense of unease lingered. The world, they realized, was a more dangerous place than they had ever imagined.

"Simple surveillance to keep up with foreign adversaries," Jack said, his voice a low murmur, "can lead to some pretty unexpected findings."

Ben nodded in agreement. They had learned a valuable lesson: in the shadowy world of intelligence, the most unexpected discoveries often lurked beneath the surface, waiting to be unearthed.

TREES

The warm afternoon sun streamed through the living room window, casting a golden glow on the antique oak table where Jack sat. He'd traded his usual dossiers and intelligence reports for something far more personal – a large sheet of white paper and a set of colorful markers.

He was sketching out a family history chart for his nephew, a bright-eyed teenager who had bombarded him with questions about their ancestry at the last Thanksgiving gathering. The child, fascinated by genealogy, had been particularly intrigued by the Dolans, a network of immigrants who had come to the United States in the 19th century during the Irish potato famine.

As Jack meticulously filled in the boxes with names, dates, and places, his mind drifted. Building relationship maps was a crucial part of his work at the CIA. He spent countless hours analyzing intricate webs of connections, deciphering the motivations of foreign leaders, and identifying potential threats.

He thought about the parallels between mapping family trees and mapping international relations. Both required meticulous attention to detail, an understanding of human behavior, and the ability to recognize patterns and connections that might not be immediately apparent. Just as a family tree revealed hidden secrets, betrayals, and unexpected alliances, so too did the intricate web of international relationships.

He remembered a case from a few years back, involving a suspected spy ring operating out of Eastern Europe. The initial investigation had yielded little, a frustrating maze of dead ends. But then, Jack had stumbled upon a seemingly insignificant detail: a photograph of the suspected ringleader with a prominent Russian oligarch, a man who, unbeknownst to most, was the oligarch's distant cousin.

That single connection, that unexpected branch on the "family tree" of international intrigue, had opened a new avenue of investigation, ultimately leading to the dismantling of the entire spy ring.

Jack smiled, a touch of amusement in his eyes. It seemed his hobby of genealogy had inadvertently sharpened his analytical skills, honed his ability to connect the dots, and perhaps even saved a few lives. He continued his work, the sun-dappled living room a world away from the shadowy realm of international espionage, yet strangely connected to it all.

The walls of Jack's office at Langley seemed to close in on him as he stared at the sprawling network map. It wasn't a family tree this time, but a complex web of individuals: Chinese diplomats, suspected spies, economists, the spouses of diplomats, and even frequent business visitors. Each name was a node, connected by a thousand invisible threads – social media interactions, financial transactions, travel records, and whispered conversations intercepted by the Agency.

Jack focused on three individuals who particularly intrigued him.

- **Li Wei:** A charming, unassuming graduate student at a prestigious university in New York. Li Wei excelled academically, publishing papers on cutting-edge technology and forging strong ties with professors. But his extracurricular activities were far more intriguing. He frequented high-end social events, cultivating relationships with venture capitalists and tech executives. Jack suspected Li Wei was gathering intelligence on emerging technologies, perhaps even seeking to recruit talent for Chinese research programs.

- **Chen Mei:** A seemingly innocuous researcher at a think tank in Washington D.C., Chen Mei specialized in US-China relations. Her public persona was that of an objective scholar, but Jack suspected a deeper agenda. Her husband, a successful businessman in New York, had leveraged his connections to gain access to sensitive financial data. Jack believed Chen Mei was subtly feeding her husband information gleaned from her research, creating a dangerous confluence of academic and commercial espionage.

- **Zhao Lin:** A mid-level official at the Chinese Embassy, Zhao Lin presented a picture of routine diplomatic work. But

Jack's investigation revealed a more intricate reality. Zhao Lin's sister-in-law, a renowned pianist, had toured extensively in the US, building a network of influential contacts in the arts and political circles. Jack suspected Zhao Lin was exploiting these connections for intelligence gathering, using his sister-in-law's social calendar as a covert operational platform.

As Jack reviewed the ever-changing Chinese network, a sense of unease settled over him. The lines between legitimate activities and espionage were blurring. The Chinese, he realized, were masters of "blending," seamlessly integrating intelligence gathering into seemingly innocuous social and professional interactions.

Shifting his attention to the Russian network proved even more challenging. The intricate web of connections was far more opaque, shrouded in a layer of secrecy and disinformation. Many names were difficult to verify, their identities obscured by aliases and complex family structures. Jack noted a significant increase in the number of Russian nationals traveling to the US under assumed identities, making it nearly impossible to track their movements and activities.

As the day wore on, Jack concluded that while the Agency had a good historical record of understanding foreign relations, the rapidly evolving global landscape presented a significant challenge. The constant flux of individuals entering and leaving the US, the proliferation of social media, and the sophistication of foreign intelligence services made it increasingly difficult to maintain a comprehensive and accurate picture of the threats facing the nation.

He knew this was just the tip of the iceberg. The shadows held countless other players, each with their own motivations and agendas. The challenge, Jack realized, was to stay ahead of the curve, to anticipate the enemy's next move, and to protect the nation from those who sought to do it harm.

Jack hunched over his workstation, the hum of the ventilation system a constant drone in the background. He was deep in the bowels of the Agency's vast computer system, a labyrinth of interconnected databases and firewalls. His latest project: to map the intricate web of relationships between individuals across multiple countries, a daunting task that felt like trying to untangle a thousand miles of fishing line.

He began by cross-referencing birth records, a painstaking process that involved deciphering archaic handwriting, translating foreign languages, and reconciling conflicting data. He then moved on to travel records, meticulously tracking the movements of individuals across borders, identifying patterns of travel and potential points of contact.

Government records proved to be a rich source of information, but also a minefield of inconsistencies and redactions. Marriages were particularly challenging, with names often changing due to cultural norms, conversions, or attempts at concealment. Jack spent countless hours chasing leads, often finding himself on a wild goose chase, only to discover a dead end.

One particularly complex relationship map involved individuals with ties to Thailand, Laos, Vietnam, and China. The connections were intricate, a tangled knot of familial and professional relationships that stretched across continents and decades. Jack meticulously traced each thread, uncovering hidden alliances, long-buried feuds, and unexpected betrayals.

Then, a breakthrough. He had been working on a particular connection for months, a seemingly insignificant link between two individuals who kept appearing on his radar. One was a businessman from Thailand, the other a retired professor from China. They had no obvious connection, no shared business ventures, no known social interactions. But then, Jack noticed something peculiar: both men consistently vacationed at the same exclusive resort in Bali, often staying in adjacent rooms.

Intrigued, Jack delved deeper. He discovered that the Thai businessman was the cousin of a cousin of the Chinese professor's wife. A seemingly insignificant detail, yet it provided a critical piece of the puzzle. It explained the inexplicable co-occurrence of these individuals in seemingly unrelated locations. It was a perfect match, a testament to the power of meticulous research and the unexpected ways in which seemingly disparate pieces of information can connect.

Exhausted but exhilarated, Jack leaned back in his chair, the glow of the computer screen reflecting in his eyes. He had unraveled another strand of the intricate web, a small victory in the ongoing battle against those who sought to exploit the vulnerabilities of a complex and interconnected world.

Jack returned to work on the problem the next morning, the revelation of the connection between the Thai businessman and the Chinese professor still buzzing in his mind. He knew this wasn't just a coincidence; it was the missing piece of the puzzle he'd been struggling to assemble.

He revisited their travel records, meticulously scrutinizing every trip, every hotel stay. And there it was – a pattern emerged. While their annual Bali vacations were their most consistent rendezvous, they also met in the US, often under the guise of family visits. The Thai businessman's son was studying at a university in California, while the Chinese professor's daughter was pursuing a PhD in New York. These "family visits" provided a perfect cover for covert meetings, allowing the men to exchange information, coordinate activities, and maintain their clandestine connection.

Further investigation revealed that these two men, through their families and extended networks, had become influential figures within their respective embassies in Washington D.C. The Thai businessman's brother-in-law was a high-ranking diplomat, while the Chinese professor's nephew was a rising star in the embassy's intelligence wing. This intricate web of familial and professional connections provided a crucial conduit for the exchange of intelligence between the two nations.

Jack realized that this discovery had profound implications. It explained the inexplicable connection between the Chinese and Thai intelligence operations in the US, a connection that had long puzzled analysts. These two men, seemingly ordinary individuals with unassuming lives, were the linchpins of a sophisticated espionage network, operating in plain sight.

As the realization sunk in, Jack poured himself a small whiskey from the small stash in his desk drawer. It was a rare moment of triumph, a testament to the power of meticulous research and the importance of persistence. He knew that these seemingly "boring" investigative techniques, the painstaking cross-referencing of data, the tireless pursuit of seemingly insignificant details, were the keys to unraveling the most complex of conspiracies.

This discovery, he knew, would have a significant impact on the Agency's operations. It would allow them to better understand the evolving threat landscape, to identify and neutralize foreign intelligence networks operating within the US, and to safeguard national security in an increasingly interconnected world. He raised his glass, a silent toast to the power of perseverance and the satisfaction of a job well done.

PEN

The flickering lights of the CIA's clandestine training room at Langley cast long, skeletal shadows across the room. Jack Dolan sat hunched over a small, metal table, his brow furrowed in concentration. Between his fingers, he held a fine-tipped brush, loaded with a colorless, odorless liquid. On the pristine white paper before him, he carefully traced the outline of a stylized bird, a symbol agreed upon by a network of clandestine operatives.

This wasn't his usual domain of data analysis and intelligence reports. This was a foray into the shadowy world of dead drops, a time-honored method of covert communication where messages were left in hidden locations for retrieval by designated individuals. Invisible ink, a relic of Cold War espionage, was making a resurgence, favored by those who sought to operate in the shadows, leaving no digital trace.

Jack practiced with meticulous care, each stroke deliberate, each line perfectly executed. He understood the importance of subtlety, of blending into the background, of leaving no trace. A smudged line, an uneven application of the ink, could compromise an entire operation, expose an agent, and jeopardize lives.

He moved on to more complex messages, short coded phrases, encrypted coordinates. Each message was a challenge, a test of his patience, his precision, and his ability to remain calm under pressure. He knew that in the real world, the stakes would be far higher. A single mistake could have devastating consequences.

As he worked, his mind drifted back to his family history research. The parallels between genealogy and intelligence gathering were becoming increasingly apparent. Both required meticulous attention to detail, an understanding of human behavior, and the ability to recognize patterns and connections that might not be immediately apparent. Just as a family tree revealed hidden secrets and unexpected alliances, so too did the intricate web of international relationships.

He thought about the challenges of mapping these hidden networks, of identifying the invisible threads that connected individuals and organizations. It was like piecing together a jigsaw puzzle with missing pieces, working with fragments of information, trying to discern the larger picture.

He knew that this practice was just the beginning. The world of espionage was constantly evolving, adapting to new technologies and new threats. He had to stay ahead of the curve, to anticipate the enemy's next move, to ensure the safety and security of the nation.

As he packed up his equipment, a sense of purpose filled him. He was a guardian, a protector, a guardian of the nation's secrets. And in this ever-changing world, he was determined to be the best at what he did.

The next morning, Jack returned to his office, the faint scent of the invisible ink still lingering on his hands. He pulled up the case file on a suspected Chinese intelligence ring operating out of San Francisco and connected to DC. The initial investigation had yielded little, a frustrating maze of dead ends. But Jack had a hunch, a feeling that this case was connected to the invisible ink training he had undergone.

He began his investigation, meticulously reviewing travel records, financial transactions, and social media activity. He searched for anomalies, for patterns that didn't quite fit, for any indication of clandestine communication. He knew that the answers, if they existed, would be hidden in plain sight, disguised as mundane activities, buried beneath layers of deception.

He spent the next few days poring over the data, his mind constantly searching for connections, for clues, for anything that could lead him to the heart of the operation. He was determined to crack this case, to bring these shadowy figures to justice. He knew that the fate of the nation might depend on it.

Jack stared at the whiteboard, a tangled mess of lines and names connecting San Francisco to Washington D.C. He'd spent the last week meticulously mapping the known members of the two suspected spy rings. The San Francisco cell, led by a charismatic businessman named Chen Wei, seemed focused on infiltrating Silicon Valley, acquiring cutting-edge technology. The D.C. cell, more politically oriented, appeared to be cultivating relationships with influential politicians and lobbying groups.

Frustration gnawed at him. The connections were tenuous, circumstantial. Chen Wei and the D.C. ring leader, a suave diplomat named Li Jian, had never been seen together. Their communication methods remained elusive.

"Any luck finding a link, Jack?" his colleague Ben inquired, his voice laced with concern.

Jack shook his head, "Nothing concrete yet. It's like they operate in separate silos, yet there's definitely a connection."

He reviewed the intercepted communications: encrypted emails, coded phone calls, dead drops. Nothing concrete, just whispers and shadows. Then, a detail caught his eye. Through various connections, both Chen Wei and Li Jian seemed to be connected by their local newspapers, both receiving it in print when most of the world had moved to digital. Chen Wei had a subscription to the San Francisco Chronicle, while Li Jian favored the Washington Post.

A flicker of an idea sparked in Jack's mind. "Ben, pull up the subscriber lists for both newspapers, focusing on print subscriptions. Pull together the journalists of articles that might be connected."

Days turned into nights as Jack delved into the subscriber lists. He cross-referenced names, searched for patterns, and meticulously analyzed the articles read by individuals connected to either ring. Slowly, a chilling realization dawned on him.

Several individuals, both in San Francisco and D.C., were connected to articles written by the same select group of journalists: renowned tech columnist for the Chronicle, David Chen, and respected political commentator for the Post, Sarah Lee.

Could it be? Were these seemingly innocuous newspapers the conduit for covert communication?

Jack began to meticulously analyze the articles written by Chen and Lee. He searched for hidden messages, for coded language, for any deviation from standard journalistic practice. He scrutinized every word, every phrase, every comma, looking for clues.

He noticed that both journalists often used similar metaphors and turns of phrase. They employed subtle word choices that could be interpreted differently by those with insider knowledge. Was this deliberate? Or merely a coincidence?

Jack wasn't sure, but he was determined to find out. He began to subscribe to both newspapers, devouring every article written by Chen and Lee. He tracked their movements, their speaking engagements, their interactions with individuals connected to the suspected spy rings.

The more he investigated, the more convinced he became that these seemingly ordinary journalists were playing a crucial role in this intricate espionage operation. They were the messengers, the conduits, the invisible threads connecting the disparate pieces of this complex puzzle.

Jack knew he was on the verge of something big. But he also knew that he was treading on dangerous ground. Uncovering this operation could be incredibly risky, but he couldn't ignore the threat.

Jack had been staking out Li Jian's residence for a few days. The suburban home, nestled amongst manicured lawns and towering trees, offered the perfect facade for a diplomat. Every morning, Li Jian would emerge from his home, his crisp suit contrasting against the dewy grass, and retrieve his copy of the Washington Post from the driveway.

Jack watched, his patience wearing thin. He needed proof, something tangible to link Li Jian to the espionage ring. Surveillance alone wasn't enough.

Finally, on a Tuesday morning, he acted. As the newspaper was delivered, Jack ran by, concealed in the shadows of a nearby tree, and picked it up, and kept on running. He snatched the newspaper from the driveway so fast, he hoped no one would see.

Back at Langley, in the confines of his lab, Jack examined the newspaper with a mixture of excitement and trepidation. He knew this was a risky move, but the potential payoff was immense.

He carefully sprayed a solution over the newspaper, the same solution used to develop invisible ink. Slowly, faint lines began to appear, revealing a cryptic message:

"Project Phoenix: Silicon Valley advancements pose significant threat. Focus efforts on influencing legislation to hinder innovation. Chen Wei will provide further details. Meeting scheduled for Friday, at the Truman piano at the National Press Club."

Jack's heart pounded. This was it. Proof. The D.C. cell was directly involved in a scheme to sabotage American technological progress. Li Jian was a key player, tasked with influencing politicians to slow down American innovation, giving China a competitive edge.

The connection to the San Francisco cell was undeniable. Chen Wei, the Silicon Valley infiltrator, was providing crucial intelligence on the cutting-edge technologies being developed in the United States.

Jack immediately contacted his superiors. A briefing with the Deputy Director was scheduled for the following morning. He entered the conference room, his hands trembling slightly as he presented his findings. The Deputy Director, a seasoned veteran of the intelligence world, listened intently, her face grim.

"This is serious, Jack," the Deputy Director said, her voice grave. "If this is true, it could have devastating consequences for national security."

Jack knew this was just the beginning. The operation to dismantle this sophisticated spy ring had just begun. The stakes were high, and the enemy was cunning. But Jack, armed with his intelligence, his determination, and his unwavering belief in justice, would persist.

Jack listened as the newscaster read, "In other news, a major blow to Chinese espionage operations in the United States was dealt this week with the arrest of several individuals suspected of belonging to a spy ring operating out of Washington D.C. Simultaneously, authorities in San Francisco apprehended members of a connected cell believed to be gathering intelligence on cutting-edge technologies in Silicon Valley."

Arrests followed a lengthy investigation spearheaded by Jack, who, through meticulous analysis of seemingly innocuous sources, uncovered a sophisticated network of communication utilizing encrypted messages and coded signals hidden within articles published in major newspapers.

In the wake of the arrests, numerous US technology firms implemented enhanced security measures, limiting access to sensitive information and bolstering their defenses against foreign espionage. The incident has served as a stark reminder of the ever-evolving nature of global threats and the critical importance of vigilance in protecting national security.

Back at Langley, Jack said to his team, "I never thought I'd say this, but I guess print journalism isn't quite dead after all."

MASQUERADE

The rhythmic dip of the oars, a counterpoint to the city's pulse, was the only sound that broke the serene surface of the Potomac. Jack Dolan, his brow beaded with sweat, glided beneath the imposing shadow of the Key Bridge. The morning sun, a fiery orb, cast long reflections on the water, painting the river in hues of gold and crimson.

It was July 1st and Independence Day was just around the corner. The city was already buzzing with anticipation. The air crackled with a festive energy, a blend of patriotic fervor and the lingering echoes of Junetheenth celebrations that had recently concluded. Jack found solace in the solitude of the river, the rhythmic motion a balm for his mind, a counterpoint to the constant churn of intelligence reports and the ever-present threat that defined his life.

He navigated the narrow channel near Roosevelt Island, his gaze sweeping across the cityscape. The Washington Monument, a gleaming obelisk, pierced the morning haze. The Lincoln Memorial, bathed in the soft morning light, exuded an aura of timeless grandeur. These landmarks, symbols of American democracy, were also constant reminders of the precarious balance between freedom and security, a balance that Jack, as a CIA operative, was sworn to uphold.

As he pulled towards the boathouse, the sounds of the city began to intrude – the distant rumble of traffic, the laughter of children playing in a nearby park, the mournful cry of a seagull circling overhead. He smiled, a fleeting expression that quickly vanished. The city, with its vibrant energy and hidden depths, was a microcosm of the world he inhabited – a world of shifting alliances, veiled threats, and the constant struggle to decipher truth from deception.

Jack stepped out of the scull, his muscles aching with a pleasant fatigue. He rinsed off at a nearby dock, the cool water a welcome relief from the morning heat. As he towelled off, he glanced at his watch. Time to head back to Langley. The Fourth of July might be a time for celebration for most Americans, but for Jack, it was another day in the relentless pursuit of his duty.

The invitation arrived unexpectedly, a handwritten note tucked into a manila envelope. "Fireworks on the Fourth? My treat," it read, signed by Richard Harrison, a former college roommate and now a senior advisor at the State Department. Jack hesitated. Social gatherings weren't exactly his forte, and the thought of navigating the crowds that would inevitably descend upon the city on Independence Day filled him with a certain degree of dread.

But Rich was an old friend, a man of sharp wit and easy company. And the promise of a rooftop view, overlooking the city's grand spectacle, was too tempting to resist.

As the fireworks began to erupt, painting the night sky in a kaleidoscope of colors, Jack found himself leaning against the balcony railing, a tumbler of bourbon in his hand. Rich, ever the raconteur, pointed towards a cluster of buildings nearby.

"Did you know," he began, his voice a low murmur against the crescendo of the 1812 Overture playing softly on the radio, "that back in the war, the CIA used to operate out of that building complex there?"

Jack raised an eyebrow. "Yes. Before Langley. It was a bustling hub of activity then. Spies, codebreakers, listening posts. A far cry from the quiet museum it became."

"A museum?" Rich inquired.

"The Naval Medical Museum," Jack explained. "They even used to have a display there, believe it or not. Shrapnel from John Wilkes Booth's bullet. A rather morbid souvenir, if you ask me. A reminder of the darker side of our history, I suppose."

"Precisely," Rich agreed. "But now, look at it. A center for peace initiatives, a place where diplomats from around the world gather to discuss solutions. A symbol, perhaps, of how far we've come."

Jack gazed out at the city, now a shimmering tapestry of light and color against the inky canvas of the night sky. The fireworks continued to explode overhead, a dazzling display of patriotism and hope. He took a long sip of his bourbon, the warmth spreading through him.

For a fleeting moment, a genuine smile touched his lips. It was a rare occurrence, a testament to the unexpected beauty of the evening, the camaraderie of old friends, and the enduring power of hope, even in the face of the world's complexities.

As the final burst of fireworks faded, leaving behind a trail of lingering smoke and the hushed murmurs of the crowd below, a figure approached Jack and Rich on the balcony. A tall, elegant woman with a warm smile, she extended a hand.

"Monsieur Dolan," she said in flawless English, her accent a melodic lilt. "Madame Dubois, French Embassy. It was a magnificent display, wasn't it?"

Rich, ever the social butterfly, introduced himself and engaged Madame Dubois in a lively conversation about the festivities. Jack, however, felt a jolt of surprise. How did she know his name?

Madame Dubois, seemingly sensing his surprise, smiled enigmatically. "Bastille Day is just around the corner," she continued, "and I wanted to extend a personal invitation to you, Monsieur Dolan. Join us at the embassy for a celebration. I assure you, it will be lively."

Jack hesitated. "Madame, I…"

"Consider it a reward," she interrupted, her eyes twinkling. "A small token of appreciation from your many friends around the world."

The implication was clear. Madame Dubois knew exactly who he was, what he did. Jack felt a shiver down his spine, a mixture of unease and a strange sense of exhilaration.

"I… I would be honored to attend, Madame," he finally replied.

Madame Dubois raised a glass of champagne that had materialized from thin air. "To friendship," she declared, her voice rich and resonant. "And to the hope that such displays of celebration will always outshine the shadows."

Jack clinked his glass against hers, a silent acknowledgement of the unspoken understanding between them. As he sipped the champagne, he couldn't help but wonder what this unexpected invitation might entail. The world of espionage, he realized, was a much smaller, and more interconnected, place than he had ever imagined.

The invitation had arrived, a simple, elegant card embossed with the French coat of arms. "Masquerade Ball," it read, in elegant calligraphy. Jack had spent the past few days preparing, a nervous energy buzzing beneath the surface. He wasn't one for social gatherings, and the prospect of mingling with diplomats and others, all cloaked in anonymity, both intrigued and intimidated him.

He settled on a costume: the Marquis de Lafayette, the French hero of the American Revolution. It seemed fitting, a nod to the historical ties that bound the two nations. He had acquired a simple white linen shirt and black breeches, complemented by a dark blue velvet jacket with gold braid. A tricorn hat, adorned with a white feather, completed the ensemble.

The pièce de résistance, however, was the mask. It was a simple, elegant creation, crafted from black velvet and edged with delicate silver filigree. The eyeholes were narrow slits, obscuring his gaze while allowing him to observe the room with a detached, almost predatory curiosity.

As the appointed hour drew near, a sense of anticipation, laced with a touch of trepidation, washed over him. He glanced at his reflection in the mirror, the mask concealing half his face. A stranger looked back at him, a figure of intrigue and mystery.

With a deep breath, Jack hailed an Uber. As the car pulled away from the curb, he adjusted the mask, a silent promise to himself to navigate the treacherous waters of the embassy ball with a cool head and a watchful eye. The night, and the secrets it held, awaited. "A l'ambassade!" he said to the driver.

The French Embassy was a spectacle. A symphony of light and shadow played across the ornate facade, casting a spell of grandeur. Inside, the air crackled with a potent mix of elegance and intrigue. Gilded cages overflowing with exotic birds added a touch of whimsy, while the scent of expensive perfume mingled with the subtle aroma of fine French wine.

Jack, navigating the throng of masked figures, felt a surge of adrenaline. This was his element, the world of shadows and intrigue. Yet, despite his years of experience, he felt a disconcerting sense of anonymity. Everyone was masked, their identities concealed, their true intentions hidden beneath the playful veneer of the masquerade.

Madame Dubois, resplendent in a gown that could have graced the shoulders of Marie Antoinette herself, approached him with a welcoming smile. "Monsieur Dolan, you are a great Lafayette!" she greeted, her voice a silken whisper. "Welcome. I trust you've found your bearings?"

Jack, feeling a flicker of unease, managed a polite nod. "Indeed, Madame. It's… quite a spectacle."

Madame Dubois, with the effortless grace of a seasoned socialite, introduced him to a whirlwind of masked figures. "Ambassador de Villiers, a connoisseur of fine wines… Madame Fontaine, a renowned art collector… Lord Harrington, a man of discerning tastes…" The names rolled off her tongue like pearls, but Jack felt a growing sense of frustration. Who were these people truly? What were their agendas?

His mind raced, trying to piece together the puzzle, to identify the faces behind the masks. But it was like trying to decipher a code written in a language he didn't understand.

Suddenly, a figure bumped into him, sending a shiver of surprise through him. A young woman, dressed in a gown strikingly similar to Madame Dubois', turned to him with an apologetic smile. "Oh, so sorry! I seem to have lost my footing."

"No harm done," Jack replied, his voice a low rumble behind the mask.

"I am Lucy," she said, her voice bright and cheerful. "Lucy Laliberte. I am Lucy the Free!"

Jack couldn't help but smile. There was a refreshing honesty about her, a genuine warmth that cut through the layers of artifice that permeated the room. He found himself relaxing, the weight of his professional anxieties momentarily forgotten.

Lucy touched his hand, her fingers lingering for a brief moment. The contact sent a jolt of unexpected warmth through him. He realized, with a sudden clarity, that amidst the intrigue and the shadows, he needed to remember to enjoy himself. After all, it was a night for freedom, a night for celebrating life.

And as the music swelled and the masked figures whirled around him, Jack Dolan, the enigmatic CIA operative, allowed himself to be swept away by the intoxicating rhythm of the night.

Jack, initially overwhelmed by the sea of masks, began to methodically read the room. He observed their movements, their gestures, the subtle nuances of their speech. The world of espionage, he realized, was a theater, and every player, no matter how well disguised, left telltale clues.

The Ambassador de Villiers, he surmised, was the man with the booming laugh and the air of effortless authority. The art collector, Madame Fontaine, was easily identified by her keen eye for detail and the almost imperceptible twitch of her wrist as she examined a particularly intricate piece of jewelry. Lord Harrington, the man of discerning tastes, could be spotted a mile away by his impeccable grooming and the way he casually dismissed the lesser wines with a flick of his wrist.

Beyond the diplomats, Jack identified other players. A man with a calculating gaze was undoubtedly a World Bank executive. A woman with a sharp tongue and a penchant for rational thought was almost certainly an IMF economist. And the man who seemed to know everyone, always hovering near the buffet, was undoubtedly one of the owners of Le Diplomate, one of the most exclusive restaurants in Washington D.C.

But it was the figures lurking in the shadows that truly piqued Jack's interest. There was the man with the hawk-like gaze and the carefully controlled movements, unmistakably Canadian. The woman with the clipped accent and the air of quiet authority, undoubtedly British. The man with the easy smile and the uncanny ability to blend into the background, an Australian, no doubt. And finally, a woman with a mischievous glint in her eye, unmistakably New Zealand.

Jack's breath hitched. The "Five Eyes," the intelligence-sharing alliance between the five Anglosphere countries. All of them were here, a silent testament to the interconnectedness of the intelligence world.

Suddenly, Lucy appeared beside him, a tray of champagne flutes in her hand. "For courage," she declared, offering him a glass. "And for navigating this treacherous sea of intrigue."

Jack took a sip, the champagne fizzing pleasantly on his tongue. "To courage, indeed," he echoed, raising his glass in a silent toast.

Lucy winked, a mischievous glint in her eye. "And to the unexpected pleasures of the evening." With a graceful curtsey, she disappeared back into the throng, leaving Jack to ponder the intricate web of connections that bound this room, and the world beyond, together.

Jack, fueled by a potent mix of champagne and intrigue, decided to play a game. He would use the masquerade as a cover, to subtly guide the "Five Eyes" towards a specific location within the embassy. He began his game, approaching each spy individually, his voice a low murmur behind his mask.

To the Canadian, he whispered, "Find the symbol of a nation born in rebellion."

To the British, he murmured, "Seek the key that unlocked a cage of tyranny."

To the Australian, he said, "Discover the relic of a day that ignited a flame of freedom."

To the New Zealander, he whispered, "Uncover the treasure that binds us to a shared history of liberty."

Each riddle, seemingly innocuous, held a specific meaning. He believed that the spies, with their sharp minds and honed instincts, would eventually connect the dots. The answer, of course, lay in the embassy's display of historical artifacts – the key to the Bastille, a symbol of French revolution and a shared legacy of freedom among the Western democracies.

Jack, having planted the seeds, circulated amongst the guests, observing their reactions. The Canadian, he noticed, was examining a collection of early history artifacts. The British woman was engrossed in a display of antique firearms. The Australian seemed drawn to a collection of art. The New Zealander, however, was already moving towards the center of the room, where a glass case displayed a collection of historical relics.

Jack, watching from a discreet distance, saw the New Zealander stop abruptly in front of the display case. Her eyes, magnified by the mask, widened slightly as she gazed upon the object within – a tarnished iron key, inscribed with intricate symbols.

One by one, the other spies, seemingly drawn by an invisible force, gravitated towards the display case. They stood in a loose circle, examining the key with a mixture of curiosity and intrigue. Jack, watching from the periphery, felt a surge of satisfaction, a knowing smile playing on his lips. The masquerade, he realized, was more than just a social occasion. It was a stage, a theater for intrigue, where even the most carefully orchestrated plans could be subtly manipulated.

The key to the Bastille, a symbol of freedom and revolution, was now at the center, transcending the boundaries of the masquerade and extended into the shadowy world of international espionage.

Jack, observing the intrigued expressions on the faces of the assembled spies, decided it was time to reveal what he had done. He approached the group, his voice a low murmur.

"Fascinating, isn't it?" he began, his gaze sweeping over the assembled spies. "The echoes of history, reverberating through the present."

The Canadian, a glint of amusement in his eyes, raised an eyebrow. "Indeed, Jack, I believe?"

Jack smiled. "Precisely. And you are, I presume, Davies, from our friends up north."

A ripple of laughter passed through the group. The British woman, her mask slipping slightly, chuckled, "Well played, Jack. Though I must admit, I fell for the art. Croft, at your service," she added, extending a hand.

The Australian, a mischievous grin playing on his lips, tipped his hat. "Riley, pleased to make your acquaintance, Jack."

The New Zealander, her eyes sparkling with amusement, simply nodded. "Bell. And you, Jack, have a knack for the dramatic."

Jack bowed his head in mock humility. "Just trying to keep things interesting."

The air crackled with a shared sense of camaraderie, a silent acknowledgment of the intricate dance just performed.

Madame Dubois, who had been observing the scene with a knowing smile, approached the group. "A most entertaining display, gentlemen and ladies," she remarked. "Your skills are truly impressive."

Lucy, appearing as if by magic, offered each of them a refill of their champagne. "To liberty, equality, and fraternity!" she declared, raising her glass.

The spies, joined by Jack and Madame Dubois, echoed the sentiment, their glasses clinking in a toast. The masquerade, once a stage for intrigue and deception, had become a celebration of shared purpose, a reminder that despite their differences, they were united by a common goal: to safeguard the freedoms that had been so hard-won.

As the night wore on, the air in the embassy grew lighter, the initial tension replaced by a sense of camaraderie and mutual respect. Jack, surrounded by his colleagues from the intelligence community, felt a sense of satisfaction. He had played his part, a small but significant role in a larger game, a game that would continue to unfold, long after the last notes of music had faded and the last guest had departed.

TURN

The flickering candlelight cast long, dancing shadows across the worn leather of his armchair. Jack Dolan, a man whose life was now a tapestry woven with threads of secrecy and danger, found himself lost in a reverie, his mind drifting back to the carefree days of his college years.

He had been a curious student, a restless spirit drawn to the intellectual buffet laid out before him. Science and engineering had been his formal pursuits, the bedrock of his understanding of the world. But his insatiable thirst for knowledge had led him down many other paths. He had delved into the intricacies of literature, exploring the nuances of language and the power of storytelling. Economics had piqued his interest, revealing the invisible forces that shaped societies and economies. And politics, the endless debates, the passionate arguments, the intoxicating thrill of dissecting power structures and understanding the levers of influence.

It was in those eclectic pursuits, Jack realized now, that he had truly honed the skills that would later prove invaluable in his career as a spy. The ability to connect seemingly disparate fields of knowledge, to see the interconnectedness of things, was paramount. A good spy, he understood, had to be an interdisciplinary actor, never feeling that any subject was too distant or too hard to observe or learn.

He had never been a model student, not in the traditional sense. His grades, while respectable, were not exceptional. He had spent more time in coffee shops, debating philosophy with his friends, than he had in the library, nose buried in textbooks. He had pursued adventures, both intellectual and physical, seeking out experiences that would broaden his horizons and deepen his understanding of the world.

And now, looking back, he realized that those "distractions" had been his greatest education. They had given him a breadth of knowledge, a depth of understanding, and a resilience that no textbook could ever provide. He had learned to think critically, to question assumptions, to see the world from multiple perspectives. He had learned to adapt, to improvise, to survive.

A soft smile touched his lips. He reached for the old, leather-bound Latin textbook that lay on the coffee table, a relic from his undergraduate days. Dusting it off, he opened it to a worn page and began to read, the rhythmic flow of the ancient language a soothing balm to his restless mind.

"Amo, amas, amat..." he murmured, declining nouns and conjugating verbs, a familiar ritual that transported him back to a simpler time, a time of intellectual exploration and youthful exuberance.

The past, he realized, was never truly gone. It lived on in the memories, in the skills, in the very essence of who he was. And as he reviewed old textbooks, Jack knew that he was not just revisiting the past, but preparing himself for the challenges that lay ahead. The world, he understood, was a complex and ever-changing landscape, and a spy, like a scholar, must always be learning, always evolving, always ready to face the unknown.

The white walls of Jack's office seemed to amplify the tension in the air as the Deputy Director entered, her face etched with a seriousness that belied her usual jovial demeanor.

"Jack," she began, her voice grave, "we've been picking up a lot of chatter lately. Things we can't quite put our finger on. But it all seems to be emanating from the college campuses around D.C."

Jack leaned forward, intrigued. "College campuses, you say? What kind of chatter?"

"Everything from recruitment attempts to… well, let's just say there's a lot of activity we can't explain," she replied, her gaze fixed on Jack's. "You're our resident expert on D.C. spy rings. I need you to take a closer look at this. See what's going on."

Jack nodded, a thoughtful expression on his face. "Universities have always been fertile ground for intelligence gathering, both for us and for our adversaries," he acknowledged. "Many of our best agents were recruited from those very campuses. But they're also vulnerable."

"Precisely," she agreed. "Young people, eager to explore, open to new ideas. They travel freely, have access to a wealth of information, and often have a lot of free time on their hands. And let's be honest, it's not always easy to distinguish between genuine academic pursuits and other activities."

"I understand the concern," Jack said, "But where do we even begin?"

"Anywhere you think is best," she replied. "Use your resources, your instincts. But be discreet. We don't want to spook anyone, not yet."

With that, she rose to leave. "I'll leave you to it, Jack. I expect a full report soon."

Jack watched her go, a thoughtful expression on his face. This was a delicate operation. He needed a team, a team of analysts, tech experts, and field agents, all with the discretion and the skills to navigate the complexities of the academic world.

He picked up the phone, a plan already forming in his mind. "Gather the team," he instructed, his voice firm. "We have a new assignment. And it's going to be a challenging one."

The next few hours were a whirlwind of activity. Jack assembled his team, a diverse group of individuals, each with their own unique skillset. There was Anya, the tech whiz, who could hack into any system imaginable. Ben, the analyst, whose mind was a veritable database of information. And Chloe, the field agent, a chameleon who could blend seamlessly into any environment.

"The objective," Jack explained, addressing his team, "is to understand the nature of this activity, to identify any potential threats, and to determine whether there are any foreign actors involved."

"Where do we start?" Ben inquired.

"We start by mapping the connections," Jack replied. " Students, professors, and visitors to these campuses. We analyze their social media, their travel history, their financial transactions. We look for patterns, for anomalies, for anything that doesn't quite fit."

"And what about the students themselves?" Chloe asked. "How do we approach them?"

"Discreetly," Jack emphasized. "We need to build trust, to become part of their world without raising any suspicions. We need to be observers, not participants."

The team, energized by the challenge, began their work. The investigation had just begun, and Jack knew that the answers they sought were likely hidden in plain sight, buried beneath layers of seemingly innocuous information.

The stakes, he realized, were high. The future of the nation, and perhaps the world, might depend on their ability to unravel the mysteries that lurked within the hallowed halls of academia.

The team had spent the last few days hunched over desks, meticulously piecing together a complex puzzle. Jack had created intricate relationship maps for each of the major universities in the D.C. area, meticulously charting the connections between students, faculty, and staff. He had mapped their social circles, their extracurricular activities, their online presence. He had cross-referenced this data with the movements of known diplomats, politicians, and intelligence officers operating in the region.

He had also meticulously mapped travel patterns – who was coming to D.C., from where, and for what purpose. He had analyzed visa applications, flight manifests, and even hotel reservations, searching for any anomalies, any patterns that didn't quite fit. The result was a sprawling, interconnected web of data, a digital tapestry that captured the vibrant social and intellectual life of the region.

But data, Jack knew, was just information. It was the interpretation of that data, the ability to see the forest for the trees, that would ultimately lead to answers.

He decided to brief the Deputy Director. "We've gathered a significant amount of data, Director," he began, "a comprehensive picture of the social and academic landscape of the region."

She nodded, her eyes gleaming with anticipation. "Any luck?"

"And now," Jack continued, "the real work begins. We need to analyze this data, to identify patterns, to understand the relationships, to see who is talking to whom, who is influencing whom."

She leaned forward, intrigued. "Any initial observations?"

Jack hesitated. "It's still early days, but there are some interesting connections emerging. Some unexpected overlaps between academic circles and certain diplomatic missions."

Her eyes narrowed. "Intriguing. Keep me informed, Jack. I want to know the moment you have something concrete."

"Of course, Director," Jack replied.

As she left, Jack turned his attention back to the data, a sense of excitement bubbling within him. The puzzle was starting to take shape, the pieces slowly falling into place. He knew that unraveling this mystery would require patience, persistence, and a keen eye for detail. But he was confident that his team, working together, would eventually uncover the truth, no matter how deeply buried it might be.

As Jack delved deeper into the data, a peculiar pattern began to emerge. While students from all corners of the globe flocked to the D.C. area universities, a disproportionate number of highly motivated individuals hailed from the Middle East and Africa.

This intrigued him. These regions, often plagued by instability, poverty, and conflict, typically had younger populations. The students arriving in D.C. were the same age as the others, but they were driven and seemingly eager to succeed quickly.

Jack saw a dichotomy. On the one hand, he recognized the "animal spirit" of development – individuals driven by adversity, seeking knowledge and opportunity to escape their circumstances. This was a force for good, a testament to the human spirit's resilience.

But a nagging unease lingered. These individuals, yearning for success, could also be vulnerable to exploitation. Desperate for a better future, they might be susceptible to recruitment by foreign actors, lured by promises of power, wealth, or a chance to bring about change in their homelands, even if those changes were destabilizing.

As he sifted through the data, a specific cluster of students caught his attention. Three individuals, all cousins, had enrolled in the same university. Their social media profiles, while seemingly innocuous, were rife with commentary on the instability of the world, the injustices they perceived, and the need for radical change. They also had documented interactions with officials from their respective embassy, suggesting a degree of influence or affiliation.

This may not be a coincidence, he thought. This was a pattern, a potential threat.

He turned to Chloe, his eyes fixed on the screen. "Chloe, I want you to take a closer look at these three students. Discreetly, of course. Observe their interactions, their social circles, their online activity. See if you can find any connection that might be of interest."

Chloe, her eyes gleaming with anticipation, nodded.

Jack watched her go, a sense of urgency growing within him. The stakes were high. These young individuals, driven by ambition and a desire for a better future, could become unwitting pawns in a dangerous game, their hopes and dreams exploited for nefarious purposes.

He knew that uncovering the truth would be a delicate operation, a dance on the edge of a precipice. But the fate of these students, and perhaps even the stability of the region, might depend on his team's ability to navigate this treacherous terrain.

Chloe returned to Langley, her face etched with a mixture of concern and intrigue. "They're complicated, Jack," she began, settling into her chair. "The three cousins. Seemingly normal, even a bit idealistic. Very passionate about their home country, understandably so. Their world is in turmoil."

Jack leaned forward, his attention focused on Chloe. "Tell me more."

"Their parents," Chloe continued, "are all prominent figures – government officials, academics. They're well-connected, influential. These kids, they're not just students. They're the future of their country, whether they like it or not."

"And what about their online activity?" Jack pressed.

"Mostly political commentary," Chloe explained. "Outrage over the instability, calls for change. But nothing concrete, no plans, no incitement to violence. More frustration, really. They feel lost, disillusioned."

Jack felt a wave of relief wash over him. "So, no immediate threat?"

"Not that I can see," Chloe confirmed. "They're more confused and upset than dangerous, at least for now."

Jack nodded. "Alright, good. But we can't afford to lose sight of them. They have the potential to be significant players in their respective countries. Powerful players."

Later that day, Jack briefed the Deputy Director. "We've identified a group of interest, Director," he reported, "three cousins, all studying at the local university. They're intelligent, well-connected, and potentially influential figures in their home country."

She raised an eyebrow. "And the threat level?"

"Minimal, for now," Jack replied. "But we need to keep an eye on them. They could become valuable assets, one way or another."

She pondered this for a moment. "Assets, you say? Interesting. I want you to engage them, Jack. Cultivate them. See if there's a way to guide them, shall we say? Start with the elder cousin."

Jack felt a flicker of unease. "Guide them? You mean recruit them?"

She smiled, a knowing glint in her eyes. "Let's just say, explore all possibilities. See if they might be interested in collaborating with us. In helping to shape the future of their country, in a way that benefits both of us."

Jack understood. She was suggesting that they turn these young, idealistic students into assets for the CIA. It was a delicate proposition, fraught with ethical considerations. But he also recognized the potential benefits. These individuals, with their deep-rooted connections and their inherent understanding of their country, could provide invaluable intelligence.

"I'll see what I can do, Director," Jack replied, a thoughtful expression on his face.

The meeting was discreet, a quiet cafe tucked away in a corner of the college. Jack, dressed in casual attire, observed the elder cousin, Omar, from across the room. Omar, despite his youthful appearance, exuded an air of quiet intensity, his eyes constantly scanning the surroundings, assessing the situation.

Jack approached, extending a hand. "Omar, isn't it? I'm, well, let's just say I'm an admirer of your work."

Omar, surprised, cautiously shook his hand. "My work?"

Jack gestured vaguely towards the table. "Your essays, your activism. You have a powerful voice, Omar. You see things clearly. I am Jack, I am a CIA agent, I want to help you."

Omar hesitated, then nodded. "The world is… broken. My country, it's suffering. The corruption, the violence, it's destroying everything."

Jack leaned forward, his voice a low murmur. "I understand. I've seen the reports. But you know, change doesn't happen overnight. It requires patience, strategy, and coordination."

Omar's eyes narrowed. "What do you mean?"

Jack took a deep breath. "Imagine a gardener, Omar. He doesn't simply uproot the weeds. He nurtures the soil, strengthens the roots of the healthy plants, and slowly, patiently, eliminates the unwanted growth."

Omar remained silent, studying Jack intently.

"We," Jack continued, "we can help you cultivate that growth. We can provide you with the resources, the information, the support you need to make a real difference in your country. To build a better future for your people."

Omar's eyes widened. "But... how? What do you want in return?"

Jack leaned back, a thoughtful expression on his face. "We believe in your potential, Omar. We believe you can be a force for positive change. And we believe that a strong, stable country is in the best interests of both our countries."

He paused, letting the weight of his words sink in. "Think of it as an investment, Omar. An investment in the future of your country, in the future of the world. We offer you safety, resources, and the opportunity to make a real impact. In return, you provide us with insights, with information that can help us understand and navigate the complexities of your region."

Omar remained silent for a long moment, his mind racing. The stakes were high, the risks immense. But the allure of the offer, the promise of power, of making a real difference, was undeniable.

Finally, he looked at Jack, a steely resolve hardening his gaze. "I accept," he said, his voice firm. "But on one condition."

Jack leaned forward, intrigued. "And what is that?"

"I want to know," Omar said, "that this is about more than just intelligence gathering. This is about building a better world, a world where freedom and justice prevail."

Jack smiled, a genuine smile. "I agree, Omar. This is about more than just intelligence. It's about building bridges, fostering understanding, creating a future where our two nations can work together, not as adversaries, but as partners."

He extended his hand. "Welcome aboard, Omar. My colleagues will contact you soon."

Omar shook his hand, a silent acknowledgment of the bargain they had just struck. The game had changed, the stakes had been raised. And as Jack watched Omar leave the cafe, he knew that the future of their relationship, and perhaps the future of their world, would be determined by the choices they made from that moment on.

SIGINT

The air in the classroom was thick with the scent of anxiety and anticipation. Jack Dolan, a seasoned veteran of the Agency, found himself surrounded by a sea of young faces, their eyes wide with a mixture of excitement and apprehension. He was back in the classroom, attending a refresher course on signal intelligence, a world that had evolved dramatically since his initial training.

Gone were the days of intercepting Morse code and deciphering handwritten ciphers. Now, the focus was on the digital domain – the vast ocean of data flowing through networks, the whispers of conversations carried on encrypted channels, the invisible trails left by every online interaction.

Jack, despite his years of experience, felt a pang of self-doubt. These young analysts, fresh out of university, were digital natives, born into a world of interconnected devices and constantly evolving technologies. They were fluent in the languages of code, adept at navigating the labyrinthine pathways of the internet. He, on the other hand, felt like a relic, a dinosaur struggling to keep pace with the accelerating pace of technological change.

Their instructor, Ava, was a force of nature. A prodigy in computer science, she had traded the ivory towers of Princeton for the less glamorous, but arguably more impactful, world of intelligence gathering. Her lectures were a whirlwind of information, a torrent of technical jargon that washed over the class like a tidal wave.

The lights dimmed, casting the classroom in a soft, ethereal glow. Ava, her voice now a low murmur, began to unpack the core concepts of signal intelligence.

"At its heart," she explained, "signal intelligence is about understanding the unseen, about extracting meaning from the noise. It's about intercepting and analyzing communications, whether they be verbal, written, or electronic, to gain an understanding of an adversary's intentions, capabilities, and vulnerabilities."

She paused, allowing her words to sink in. "Think of it as a vast ocean of information," she continued, her voice gaining intensity, "a cacophony of voices, a symphony of signals. Our job is to isolate the relevant signals, to filter out the noise, to decipher the hidden messages within."

Ava then delved into the leading theories that guided their work. "There's the

Shannon-Weaver model, which focuses on the transmission of information through a channel. Then there's game theory, which helps us understand the strategic interactions between adversaries. And of course, there's the ever-evolving field of social network analysis, which allows us to map the relationships between individuals and organizations."

She illustrated her points with vivid examples, drawing on historical events and contemporary challenges. "During World War II," she explained, "breaking the Enigma code was a turning point in the war. Today, we face new challenges – the rise of encryption, the proliferation of dark web marketplaces, the constant evolution of cyber warfare."

"But the fundamental principles remain the same," she emphasized. "It's about understanding human behavior, about anticipating their actions, about anticipating their intentions. It's about connecting the dots, about seeing the bigger picture."

Jack found himself completely absorbed, his mind racing with possibilities. He envisioned a world of interconnected networks, a vast tapestry of information, where every keystroke, every phone call, every online interaction left a digital footprint. The challenge, he realized, was to make sense of this overwhelming volume of data, to extract the critical intelligence that could shape the course of history.

As Ava continued her lecture, painting a vivid picture of the challenges and rewards of signal intelligence, Jack felt a renewed sense of purpose. He was ready to embrace the future, to learn, to adapt, to continue his lifelong pursuit of truth in the ever-changing landscape of the intelligence world.

Ava, sensing the rapt attention of her audience, delved deeper into the Shannon-Weaver model. "Think of it like this," she began, sketching a simple diagram on the whiteboard. "You have a source, which is the origin of the information – a person speaking, a computer transmitting data. This information is then encoded into a signal – a series of electrical impulses, a sequence of binary digits."

"This signal," she continued, "is then transmitted through a channel. This channel could be anything – a telephone line, a radio wave, the internet. But the channel is never perfect. There's always noise – interference, distortion, anything that can corrupt the signal."

"On the receiving end," she explained, "the signal is decoded, and the information is received by the destination. But because of the noise, the received information may not be identical to the original information."

"Our job," she concluded, "is to minimize the impact of that noise. To develop techniques that allow us to accurately decode the signal, to extract the true meaning from the corrupted data."

She paused, allowing the students to absorb the information. "This model," she emphasized, "is fundamental to our understanding of communication. It helps us understand the limitations of any communication system, and it guides our efforts to overcome those limitations."

Jack, fascinated by Ava's explanation, realized that the Shannon-Weaver model was more than just a theoretical framework. It was a practical tool, a guide for navigating the complexities of the digital world. He understood that in the ever-evolving landscape of intelligence gathering, the ability to identify and mitigate noise was paramount.

As Ava continued her lecture, exploring the various techniques used to improve signal quality and enhance data transmission, Jack felt a renewed sense of excitement. He was ready to embrace the challenge, to delve deeper into the intricacies of signal intelligence, to become a master of the noise.

Ava, sensing the class had grasped the fundamentals of the Shannon-Weaver model, shifted gears. "Now," she declared, "let's talk about game theory. This is where things get truly fascinating."

She paused for dramatic effect, then continued, "Game theory is the study of strategic decision-making in situations where the outcome for each participant depends not only on their own actions, but also on the actions of others."

Ava drew a simple diagram on the whiteboard, a 2x2 grid. "Let's take the classic example: the Prisoner's Dilemma. Two suspects are arrested for a crime. They are held in separate cells and offered a deal: if they confess and implicate their partner, they receive a reduced sentence. If they both remain silent, they receive a minor penalty. If one confesses and the other remains silent, the confessor goes free while the silent partner receives a harsh sentence."

"Now," Ava continued, "imagine this scenario played out on the world stage. Two nations, each possessing nuclear weapons, face a critical decision. Do they cooperate and disarm, reducing the risk of global annihilation, or do they pursue an arms race, risking mutual destruction?"

"Game theory helps us understand the complexities of these situations," she explained. "It allows us to predict the likely outcomes, to identify the optimal strategies for each player, and to explore the potential consequences of different choices."

Jack found himself captivated by Ava's explanation. He realized that game theory was not just an abstract concept; it was a powerful tool for understanding the dynamics of international relations, for anticipating the moves of adversaries, and for developing effective countermeasures.

"In the world of intelligence," Ava continued, "game theory is crucial. We need to understand the motivations and decision-making processes of our adversaries, to anticipate their moves, and to develop strategies that will give us the advantage."

She paused, her gaze sweeping across the class. "In essence," she concluded, "game theory is the art of deception, of anticipating and manipulating the expectations of others. It's about understanding the psychology of conflict and cooperation, and using that understanding to achieve our objectives."

Jack, his mind reeling with new insights, realized that Ava had just opened a door to a whole new world of strategic thinking. The world of intelligence, he understood, was a complex game, and mastering the principles of game theory would be crucial to success.

Ava, sensing the class was grappling with the abstract nature of game theory, shifted gears once more. "Now," she declared, "let's talk about something a bit more tangible – social networks."

She gestured towards the whiteboard, where she had sketched a simple diagram of interconnected nodes. "In the digital age," she explained, "we are all interconnected. We are part of vast, intricate networks – social networks, professional networks, even networks of devices. And these networks, believe it or not, are a goldmine of intelligence."

"Social network analysis," she continued, "allows us to map these connections, to identify key influencers, to understand the flow of information within a group. We can analyze patterns of communication, identify clusters of individuals with shared interests, and even predict future behavior."

Ava gave a few compelling examples. "Imagine a terrorist organization," she said. "By analyzing their online activity – their social media posts, their online forums, their encrypted communications – we can map their network, identify their leaders, and predict their next move."

"Or consider a foreign intelligence service," she continued. "By analyzing their recruitment patterns, their communication channels, and their interactions with potential agents, we can identify their vulnerabilities and disrupt their operations."

Jack was fascinated. He realized that social network analysis was not just about tracking friends and family on social media. It was about understanding the dynamics of power, the flow of information, and the hidden connections that shaped the world around us.

"In the digital age," Ava concluded, "the lines between the physical and the digital world are blurring. Our online activities leave a digital footprint, a trail of breadcrumbs that can be analyzed and exploited. Understanding these networks, mastering the art of social network analysis, is crucial for anyone operating in the intelligence world today."

Jack, his mind buzzing with new insights, realized that Ava had opened his eyes to a world of interconnectedness, a world where every interaction, every online activity, had the potential to be observed, analyzed, and exploited. The challenge, he understood, was to navigate this complex web of connections, to understand the rules of the game, and to use that understanding to achieve his objectives.

As the lecture drew to a close, Jack, still grappling with the complexities of social network analysis, raised his hand. "Ava," he began, "you've painted a fascinating picture of the evolving landscape of intelligence gathering. But how do we prepare for the threats of the future? Technologies are constantly evolving, new threats are emerging every day. How do we stay ahead of the curve?"

Ava smiled, acknowledging his question. "That's the million-dollar question, Jack. The world of intelligence is a constant game of catch-up. We need to be adaptable, to be lifelong learners."

"We need to cultivate a culture of innovation," she continued, "to encourage experimentation and risk-taking. We need to invest in cutting-edge research, to develop new tools and technologies that can anticipate and counter emerging threats."

"But most importantly," she emphasized, "we need to invest in our people. We need to recruit and develop the brightest minds, individuals with diverse backgrounds and skillsets – linguists, mathematicians, computer scientists, sociologists. We need analysts who are not only technically proficient, but also possess strong critical thinking skills, cultural awareness, and an understanding of human behavior."

"The future of intelligence," she concluded, "lies in the human element. It's about harnessing the power of human ingenuity, of human intuition, to navigate the complexities of the digital age and to safeguard our national security."

Jack listened intently, absorbing Ava's words. He realized that the future of intelligence gathering would require a multi-faceted approach, a combination of technological sophistication and human ingenuity. He understood that the most valuable asset, in this ever-evolving landscape, would be the human mind, capable of critical thinking, creative problem-solving, and a deep understanding of the human condition.

As the clock hit the top of the hour in the room, signaling the end of the lecture, Jack felt a renewed sense of purpose. He was ready to embrace the challenges of the future, to hone his skills, and to contribute to the ongoing evolution of intelligence gathering in the 21st century.

GIFTS

The first rays of dawn painted the sky in hues of orange and pink, casting long, skeletal shadows across the forest floor. Jack Dolan, his breath misting in the crisp autumn air, pushed himself up the steep incline, his boots crunching on the fallen leaves. He was deep within the heart of Cunningham State Park, the vibrant greens of summer replaced by a breathtaking tapestry of reds, yellows, and oranges.

He reached the summit, gasping for breath, his heart pounding in his chest. The view was breathtaking. The rising sun, a fiery orb, bathed the valley below in a golden light. The air was still, the only sounds were the rustling of leaves and the distant call of a bird.

Jack, despite his exhaustion, felt a surge of exhilaration. This solitude, this connection with nature, was a rare treat for a man whose life was spent navigating the murky waters of the intelligence world.

But his mind, even in this moment of tranquility, was already at work. Today was the first day of a high-level diplomatic summit at Camp David. World leaders, their entourages, and countless diplomats would be converging on the secluded presidential retreat, attempting to negotiate peace in some of the world's most troubled regions.

Jack, though here for a much-needed hiking trip, had a secondary mission. He would be keeping a discreet eye on the comings and goings, observing the diplomats, identifying potential points of contact, and subtly monitoring their communications. The proximity to Washington D.C. meant that familiar faces, both friendly and unfriendly, would inevitably appear, providing him with a valuable opportunity to continue building his network and staying abreast of the latest intelligence.

He took a deep breath, the crisp air filling his lungs. The game, he knew, was always on. Even in the quiet solitude of the forest, the shadows of the intelligence world lingered, ever present, ever watchful.

Jack settled himself deeper into the shadows, his eyes trained on the winding driveway that snaked its way through the idyllic landscape of Camp David. Suburbans, sleek and anonymous, glided through the gates, depositing their occupants at the lodge or at the various cabins scattered amongst the pines. Jack watched, a silent observer, noting the arrival times, the license plate numbers, the subtle cues of body language and dress.

He was a human shadow, a ghost in the woods. His job was to observe, to listen, to piece together the puzzle of human interaction. Who was stepping out of which vehicle? Who was making the rounds, visiting multiple cabins? Who was spending extended periods in close proximity to officials? These seemingly insignificant details, when woven together, could reveal crucial information – alliances forming, disagreements brewing, and perhaps, even the seeds of future conflicts.

The air crackled with an undercurrent of tension. The weight of the world, it seemed, rested on the shoulders of the men and women gathered within those secluded cabins. The fate of nations hung in the balance, determined by the give and take of diplomatic discourse, by the subtle nuances of negotiation and compromise.

Jack witnessed a poignant exchange. A distinguished-looking diplomat, his face weathered by years of service, presented a small, intricately carved wooden eagle to a senior State Department official. A symbol of freedom, a gesture of goodwill, perhaps. The American official accepted the gift with a gracious smile, handing it to his assistant who disappeared into the lodge.

Jack felt a pang of hunger. He had been observing for hours, his stomach rumbling in protest. He decided to break for a brief respite, heading towards a small cache of supplies he had stashed earlier that day. As he moved through the undergrowth, he felt like a red fox, a solitary predator observing the movements of its prey. He was always watching, always listening, always gathering information.

As the sun began its descent, painting the sky in hues of orange and purple, Jack continued his vigil. He observed the comings and goings, noting the subtle shifts in the dynamics between the diplomats. Some remained aloof, others engaged in animated conversations, while still others seemed preoccupied, their eyes darting nervously around.

He noticed a flurry of activity around one particular cabin. A group of aides scurried in and out, their faces etched with a mixture of concern and urgency. A technician, his face pale, emerged from the cabin, clutching a laptop. Jack, intrigued, focused his attention on that particular cabin.

Suddenly, his phone vibrated in his pocket. A text message from Langley. Jack quickly checked it. "Urgent. Contact Deputy Director immediately."

He pulled out his satellite phone, the signal crackling to life. "Deputy Director," he said, his voice low. "Jack here."

"Jack," her voice was tight, "we're detecting some… unusual electronic activity emanating from Camp David."

Jack's eyebrows furrowed. "Unusual activity? What kind of activity?"

"We can't be certain yet," she replied, her voice urgent. "But it appears to be some kind of signals. We need you to investigate, discreetly, of course. See if you can determine the source and the nature of these transmissions."

Jack felt a surge of adrenaline. This was unexpected, a new wrinkle in the already complex situation. "Understood, Director. I'll be discreet. I'll keep you updated."

He disconnected the call, his gaze fixed on the cabin that had been the source of the initial disturbance. The shadows were deepening, the air growing colder. But the game, far from over, had just taken a dramatic turn. Jack, the silent observer, was now a player, drawn into the heart of the intrigue.

As the moon cast long, eerie shadows across the Camp David grounds, Jack remained vigilant. He had established a concealed observation point, the rustling leaves providing the perfect camouflage. He watched as the diplomats, weary from a long day of negotiations, retired to their sleeping cabins. The lights in the lodge flickered and died, plunging the compound into an eerie silence.

It was time to act. Jack needed to get inside, to investigate the source of the electronic transmission. He pulled out his phone and dialed a discreet number.

"Rich," Jack whispered, his voice barely audible. "It's Jack. I need your help."

A low chuckle emanated from the other end of the line. "Jack Dolan, needing my help? What kind of trouble are you in this time?"

"Nothing I can't handle," Jack replied, "but I need access to the lodge at Camp David. Discreetly, of course."

"Access to the lodge, you say?" Rich pondered for a moment. "That might be challenging. But I have a few connections."

An hour later, under the cover of darkness, Rich, his face pale but determined, slipped out of a side door of a cabin. He moved with the agility of a seasoned operative, his movements fluid and precise. "Be quick. Security sweeps are frequent with lots of different diplomats."

Jack nodded, his heart pounding. He slipped into the lodge, his senses on high alert. He moved cautiously, his eyes scanning the room. There was nothing out of the ordinary – writing desks arranged in a circle, a small sitting area.

Then, he spotted it. The wooden eagle, the gift, tucked among a wall of books. Jack raised a wand he had over the eagle and it beeped. This was no accidental signal. It was deliberate, a sophisticated attempt to communicate. It was a listening device. Jack, his mind racing, acted quickly. He grabbed the eagle and disappeared into the darkness.

The crisp air whipped through Jack's hair as he raced back to his hidden cache, his car, and on the road back to Langley. He carried the carved wooden eagle through the door and took it down to the lab.

Back at Langley, the Deputy Director joined Jack in the lab. The eagle sat on the table, an innocent-looking souvenir. The Deputy Director's face etched with concern, she gestured towards it. "Let's see what secrets this little bird holds."

Jack, using a combination of tools and finesse, carefully disassembled the eagle. Beneath the intricate carvings, hidden within the hollowed-out body, lay a miniature, yet sophisticated, transmission device. It was a marvel of engineering, designed to blend seamlessly with its surroundings.

"Bingo," she muttered. "Someone was trying to listen in on the negotiations."

A wry smile played on Jack's lips. "Looks like history has a way of repeating itself, Director."

"The Great Seal bug," Jack explained. "Back in the 1940s, the Soviets planted a listening device inside the Great Seal of the United States, right there in the ambassador's office."

She chuckled. "Seems our adversaries are still fond of the classics. Though, I must admit, this eagle is a more elegant execution than a clunky seal."

Relief washed over both of them. They had solved the mystery, averted a potential diplomatic disaster, and ensured the talks at Camp David could continue uninterrupted. The eagle, a symbol of freedom, had been used for a far more sinister purpose. But thanks to Jack's keen observation and Rich's resourceful assistance, the bird's song had been silenced.

As Jack left the lab, he couldn't help but feel a sense of satisfaction. The game of shadows, of hidden agendas and clandestine operations, was a constant challenge. But it was also a game he was determined to win, one move at a time. The world might be a complex and dangerous place, but as long as there were people like him, vigilant and dedicated, there would always be a chance for peace and security.

TUNNELS

The door to Jack's office burst open, and in strode Ben, his face alight with excitement. "Jack," he exclaimed, "I think I've stumbled upon the next great adventure."

Jack, eyebrows raised, gestured for him to continue. "Spill it, Ben. What's got you so worked up?"

Ben leaned in conspiratorially. "Remember that crazy mission we did running through the Rock Creek Park woods, trying to listen in on the backyards of those embassies?"

Jack chuckled. "How could I forget? One of my best adventures with you, Ben."

"Exactly," Ben grinned. "Well, seems the Agency is dusting off an old asset. Something we thought was lost to the ages."

Jack's curiosity was piqued. "An old asset? What are we talking about?"

Ben paused for dramatic effect. "The spy tunnel."

Jack's jaw dropped. "The tunnel under Embassy Row? The one they built during the Cold War?"

Ben nodded vigorously. "The very one. It's been abandoned for decades, declared unstable. But apparently, some old blueprints resurfaced, and someone decided to take a closer look with interest in those embassies."

Jack's mind raced. The tunnel, a relic of a bygone era, a forgotten relic of the Cold War. It was a stroke of genius, a way to eavesdrop on the embassies without ever setting foot on their property. "And what's the plan?" Jack asked, his voice barely a whisper.

Ben grinned. "To reactivate it, of course. Upgrade it, modernize it. Turn it into the ultimate listening post in the heart of D.C."

Jack felt a thrill course through him. This wasn't just any mission; this was a piece of history, a chance to resurrect a forgotten legend. "This is going to be interesting," he murmured, a mischievous glint in his eye.

The adventure, it seemed, was just beginning.

Embassy Row. The very name conjured up images of grandeur, of opulent mansions and high-stakes diplomacy. But beneath the veneer of sophistication, a darker history lurked.

Long before it became a haven for foreign dignitaries, Massachusetts Avenue was the domain of Washington D.C.'s elite. In the late 19th and early 20th centuries, the area was known as "Millionaires' Row," a testament to the extravagant mansions that lined its streets. These opulent homes, with their manicured gardens and opulent interiors, were a showcase of wealth and social status.

The advent of World War II, however, brought about a significant shift. As the United States increasingly became involved in global affairs, the need for diplomatic representation grew. Many of these grand mansions, symbols of a bygone era, were purchased by foreign governments and transformed into embassies.

The Cold War, with its escalating tensions and espionage, cast a long shadow over Embassy Row. The area became a battleground for intelligence agencies, a stage for covert operations and clandestine meetings. Spies, both foreign and domestic, lurked in the shadows, their eyes and ears ever vigilant.

The construction of the tunnel, a clandestine project shrouded in secrecy, was a testament to the paranoia and suspicion that permeated the Cold War era. It was a bold move, a desperate attempt to gain an edge on the enemy, to eavesdrop on their conversations, to anticipate their moves.

Jack, as he pondered the history of Embassy Row, felt a shiver down his spine. He was about to delve into that history, to walk in the footsteps of those who came before him, to witness firsthand the ghosts of the Cold War. The adventure, he realized, was about to become far more significant than he had initially imagined.

The row house looked deceptively ordinary. A faded brick facade, peeling paint, and overgrown ivy gave it the appearance of a neglected property. But behind that unassuming exterior lay a secret, a relic of the Cold War.

Jack and Ben, disguised as construction foremen, surveyed the property. A team of agents, posing as contractors, had been working diligently for weeks, creating the illusion of a legitimate renovation project. The Agency had discreetly purchased the property, providing the perfect cover for their clandestine operations.

"Alright, let's see what we're working with," Ben said, unfolding a set of blueprints. "According to the old records, the tunnel access point should be somewhere in this basement."

Jack peered into the dimly lit basement, dust motes dancing in the single shaft of sunlight piercing through a grimy window. "Looks like they did a thorough job of concealing it," he observed. "No obvious signs of a hidden entrance."

Ben pointed to a section of the basement floor. "The blueprints indicate a structural weakness here. A slight dip in the foundation. That's likely where they concealed the access point."

Jack nodded. "Alright, let's get to work. We need to reinforce the foundation, but subtly, without raising any suspicion."

The next few weeks were a whirlwind of activity. The "construction crew" worked tirelessly, excavating the basement, reinforcing the foundation, and installing new plumbing and electrical systems. But beneath the surface, a different kind of construction was taking place.

Jack and Ben, utilizing the latest in excavation technology, carefully probed the designated area. They used ground-penetrating radar, seismic sensors, and even a small robotic probe to map the hidden passageways beneath the surface. Slowly but surely, they began to uncover the forgotten tunnel, piece by piece.

As they delved deeper, they uncovered the ingenuity of the engineers who had built it. The tunnel, reinforced with concrete and lined with lead to shield against electronic eavesdropping, was a marvel of Cold War engineering. It was a testament to the lengths that intelligence agencies would go to gain an edge, to listen in on the whispers of their adversaries.

Jack, standing amidst the dust and debris, felt a thrill course through him. He was not just restoring a dilapidated building; he was resurrecting a piece of history, breathing new life into a forgotten relic of the Cold War.

Jack spread a large-scale map of Washington D.C. across the makeshift worktable in the basement. "Alright, Ben," he said, "let's talk strategy. We're not just going to listen in on one embassy. We're going to build a network."

He pointed to a series of locations on the map. "The Russian Embassy, the Chinese Embassy, the Iranian Embassy, these are our primary targets."

Ben nodded, tracing the lines of the tunnel system with his finger. "But how do we do it without raising suspicion? We can't exactly start digging trenches in their backyards."

Jack grinned. "That's where the beauty of this tunnel lies. We'll utilize existing infrastructure. Sewer lines, abandoned utility tunnels, there are plenty of ways to discreetly extend our reach."

He paused, his eyes narrowing. "But we need to be meticulous. We don't want to alert anyone. No vibrations, no unusual sounds. We're dealing with some of the most sophisticated intelligence agencies in the world."

Ben pointed to a section of the map. "The Cuban Embassy," he said, "That one will be tricky. Their security is notoriously tight."

Jack nodded. "Agreed. We'll need to proceed with extreme caution. No heavy machinery near their property. We'll do it by hand, if necessary."

And so, they began. Days turned into weeks, each excavation a delicate dance of precision and secrecy. They worked late into the night, the only sound the rhythmic thud of their shovels against the earth. Around the Cuban Embassy, they eschewed heavy machinery, opting for hand tools, the soft scrape of metal against stone the only sound disturbing the night.

Finally, after weeks of tireless effort, the tunnel was complete. A network of hidden listening devices, the latest in state-of-the-art surveillance technology, was installed along its length. The signals, carefully amplified and filtered, were transmitted back to Langley, where analysts would decipher the whispers of the world, the secrets whispered behind closed doors.

As the final touches were being put on the renovation project – a fresh coat of paint applied to the facade of the row house – Jack stood back and admired their handiwork. The tunnel, a relic of the past, had been reborn, a silent guardian, a watchful eye on the pulse of the world. The game, he realized, had just begun.

The renovation project on the row house finished up, a facade for the clandestine operations unfolding beneath the surface. Finally, the day arrived. In the heart of Langley, within a secure, soundproofed room, a team of analysts gathered around a bank of monitors. Jack and Ben stood side-by-side, anticipation crackling in the air.

The first transmissions began to trickle in. Static, then a faint hum, then voices.

"This is Ambassador…," a voice began, muffled but distinct. "…insist on… concessions…"

Jack and Ben exchanged a look of triumph. It was working. The tunnel, their silent guardian, was delivering on its promise.

As the hours passed, the transmissions grew clearer, the conversations more distinct. They intercepted diplomatic discussions, overheard heated arguments, and even gleaned snippets of personal conversations. The information was invaluable, a treasure trove of intelligence that provided a unique window into the inner workings of foreign embassies.

The Deputy Director, her face a mask of quiet satisfaction, entered the room. "Gentlemen," she said, raising a glass of champagne, "to a job well done. To the ghosts of the past, and the future they have helped us secure."

Jack and Ben raised their glasses in a silent toast. The tunnel, a relic of the Cold War, had been reborn, a testament to the enduring power of ingenuity and the relentless pursuit of knowledge. The game, they realized, was far from over. The whispers from beneath the streets of Washington D.C. would continue to provide invaluable insights, shaping the course of international relations for years to come.

DISAPPEAR

At Langley, the lights of the Deputy Director's office buzzed, casting a glow on her face. Her expression was grim, a stark contrast to the usually jovial demeanor.

"Jack," she began, her voice a low thrum, "your legend has grown too long. Too many eyes are on you."

Jack, his gaze fixed on the worn Persian rug, knew what was coming. Years of operating in the shadows, of pulling off impossible missions, had finally caught up with him. The whispers had started subtly – a rival agent bumping into him at a crowded market, a strange accent in the background of a phone call, a flicker of recognition in the eyes of a local official. Now, the whispers were a cacophony, threatening to drown him out.

"They know," the Deputy Director continued, "who you are, what you've done. The Russians, the Chinese, the Iranians... they all want a piece of you. You are a known asset of the CIA."

Jack remained silent, his mind racing. He had always known this day might come. The life of a ghost, of a man who existed only in the shadows, was inherently precarious.

"We're going to make you disappear," the Deputy Director said bluntly. "An accident. A plane crash, a car wreck, something believable. You'll be off the grid, Jack. No more missions, no more field work. You'll be on your own."

A wave of bitter amusement washed over him. Years of service, of risking his life for his country, and this was his reward? A phantom existence, a life lived in the shadows, even deeper than before.

"But you won't be alone, entirely," the Deputy Director added, sensing his internal turmoil. "The Agency will provide resources when needed. Discreetly, of course. But your primary directive, Jack, is survival. Protect yourself, at all costs."

Jack nodded, his voice a mere rasp. "Understood."

And so, Jack Dolan, the man who had vanished into the shadows countless times, would finally vanish. He would become a ghost, a legend whispered about in intelligence circles, a cautionary tale for those who dared to tread too deeply into the murky waters of espionage.

His primary focus now was independent survival.

The Deputy Director turned on the television.

The newscaster spoke, "In other news, a small single-engine plane crashed in the rugged mountain terrain of Alaska, west of the Canadian border, near the town of Eagle. The aircraft went down earlier today, and rescue crews have been dispatched to the scene.

However, due to the remote and treacherous nature of the terrain, officials are not optimistic about finding any survivors."

She turned off the television and closed her eyes.